The black gelding stuck his head under some rainwater falling from the top of the tarp. Sputtering, he shook his forelock and mane, spraying them all.

Taylor jumped away, laughing. "Like I'm not already wet enough, Albert!" she joked, flinging the water from her hands at him.

Albert sputtered, nodded his head, and licked his lips. Taylor was sure he was playing along. Pixie neighed cheerfully.

Oh, if she only *could* keep them! Taylor felt the desire to own them as an ache deep inside.

Was it *really* impossible?

Of course it was!

But it would be so wonderful!

What would it hurt to at least ask?

Ride over to
WILDWOOD STABLES

Daring to Dream
Playing for Keeps

WILDWOOD STABLES

Daring to Dream

BY SUZANNE WEYN

SCHOLASTIC INC.
New York Toronto London Auckland
Sydney Mexico City New Delhi Hong Kong

No part of this publication may be reproduced, stored in a retrieval system, or transmitted in any form or by any means, electronic, mechanical, photocopying, recording, or otherwise, without written permission of the publisher. For information regarding permission, write to: Scholastic Inc., Attention: Permissions Department, 557 Broadway, New York, NY 10012.

ISBN: 978-0-545-14979-2

12 11 10 9 8 7 6 5 4 3 2 1   10 11 12 13 14 15/0

Printed in the U.S.A.
First printing, March 2010

To Diana Weyn Gonzalez,
my blue-ribbon horse expert, always my darling girl.

Chapter 1

Taylor Henry rode bareback across the cornflower-strewn field of tall grass on a glistening Arabian stallion. Clutching the creature's glossy black mane, she leaned forward, gripping with her knees and thigh muscles, in a smooth rhythm with the ebony horse beneath her.

The last yellow rays of sun streaked the gathering purple-pink of the sky. The golden lines seemed as though they were trying to write her a message. In fact, she was starting to see letters forming. What did they say? She could almost make it out.

"CARE TO SHARE THAT WITH THE REST OF THE CLASS, TAYLOR?"

Taylor was pitched forward over the head of the

stallion and landed with a thud in her seat at Pheasant Valley Middle School.

· Looking down sharply, she stared at the sketch she'd been so absorbed in drawing. The field of breeze-wafted flowers was there, and so were the sunset and the majestic, racing Arabian. But all their vividness had faded back to number-two pencil gray the moment she'd been abruptly tossed out of the scene.

Looking up at her frowning teacher, she began to twirl her long brown ponytail nervously. "It's just something I was drawing," she told Mr. Romano.

Her eighth-grade social studies teacher strode down the aisle toward her. Mr. Romano was probably one of the cooler teachers at Pheasant Valley Middle School, but Taylor knew from experience that daydreamers annoyed him.

Mr. Romano lifted the sketch and quickly examined it. "Not bad," was his surprisingly mild comment. "Are you a horse enthusiast?"

"You could definitely say that."

"Is this your horse?" he asked.

Before Taylor could admit that the animal was the horse of her dreams — but only her dreams — a snort of derision erupted from across the classroom. "As if!" Plum Mason scoffed.

Taylor narrowed her eyes in the girl's direction. Plum ignored her, but the uneasy way she fussed with her sparkling diamond stud earring proved that she'd caught the look. Fluffing her long, curly blonde hair, Plum shifted in her seat. "I mean . . . a horse costs a lot of money," she explained sweetly to Mr. Romano. "Even *I* don't have one."

"And if the princess doesn't have a horse, no one else can have one, either," taunted a lanky blond boy slumped in his chair, legs sprawled into the aisle.

"Shut up, Jake!" Plum bristled hotly. "You're an idiot!"

Delighted that he'd ruffled her, Jake Richards grinned. "Poor Plum. Daddy won't buy her a pony."

Plum sneered at him. "Loser!"

"Hey! Hey!" Mr. Romano intervened forcefully. "Let's not be calling names."

"Well, he *is*," Plum mumbled.

The buzzer for the end of last class sounded, and Taylor's shoulders sagged with relief. Plum and Jake's fight had gotten her off the hook.

"Your reports are due Monday. The differences between the old and new periods of the ancient Egyptian empire," Mr. Romano shouted to the departing class. "Typed! Double-spaced!"

He handed Taylor back her sketch. "So? *Is* this your horse?"

Taylor laughed lightly but with a note of sadness. "I wish it were, but no. We could never afford a horse, especially now that . . ." She looked away, wishing she could roll back her last three words. It wasn't something she wanted to talk about.

He waited for her to continue. "Now that what?" he prompted after another moment passed.

"Nothing. It's just that a horse is way too expensive, is all. Plum was right about that."

He nodded. "But you like horses?"

"I'm crazy about them," Taylor confirmed. "All animals, really, but most of all horses. I have horse posters in my room. I read horse books. I even order horse catalogs and go online to their websites just to look at all the cool gear. Kind of weird, I know."

"And you like to draw them," Mr. Romano added.

Little red flags marked *uh-oh* popped up in Taylor's

brain. He was heading the conversation back to what she was in trouble for doing.

Taylor looked away sheepishly and nodded.

"During my class," he continued.

"I'm sorry," she apologized. "Ancient Egypt is very interesting and all, but it just seems like . . . a really long time ago."

"So it doesn't hold your attention?" he inquired.

"Not as much as horses," she said truthfully.

Mr. Romano stroked his chin. "Okay, here's your penalty for daydreaming in my class. Horses were introduced to ancient Egypt around 1700 B.C. They were used mostly for chariots by the military. I want an additional two pages about horses in ancient Egypt."

"Two *typed* pages?" Taylor squeaked in objection. "That's a lot."

He nodded. "Well, maybe it will help you keep your mind on class next time."

A heavyset boy with short-cropped, white-blond hair stuck his head into the classroom. "Taylor, you're going to miss the bus!" said Travis Ryan, Taylor's best friend.

Chapter 2

Taylor sat in one of the middle seats of the school bus with a Dover Saddlery catalog on her lap, thumbing through it and talking to Travis, seated beside her. "Look at these dressage coats — and I love the velvet helmets," she said with wistful longing. "Could you imagine me in one of those outfits?"

She could imagine it: the high white collar, formfitting jacket, and gleaming knee-high black riding boots, her long brown ponytail bundled into a net-covered bun beneath a rounded velvet helmet.

"No, it's definitely not you," Travis said, honest to a fault as always. "You're not the type. Plum Mason is more the type for that stuff."

"Why?" Taylor demanded, feeling offended for some reason she didn't fully understand. "Why should she have this stuff and not me?"

Travis shrugged. "I don't know." He pulled an X-Men graphic novel from his pack and began to peruse it. "Don't get all mad about it," he said, his eyes on the page. "It's a compliment to you, sort of."

Taylor wasn't so sure about that.

Travis looked up. "Hey, I hear Plum and Jake Richards broke up."

"Where have you been?" Taylor asked. "That's old news."

Travis went back to his graphic novel. "You know I don't pay attention to gossip."

Taylor did know. She wished she could block out this kind of drama, too. There was way too much of it in the eighth grade in her opinion.

Returning to her catalog, Taylor continued to go through it. She didn't agree with Travis. The English riding gear was graceful and elegant.

"Whoa!" Travis cried.

"What happened?" Taylor asked.

"Wolverine almost got destroyed!"

"How many of those things do you read a week?" Taylor asked.

"I don't know. It depends on how many come out that week," Travis replied.

They sat together, each reading, for the next five minutes until Travis craned his neck over to look at Taylor's catalog. She was checking out the English-style riding helmets. "Do they have cowgirl hats in there?" Travis asked. She supposed he was suggesting that a cowgirl hat was more her style. And maybe it was.

"No cowgirl hats in here," Taylor answered him. "This catalog is just English and dressage gear."

"Then why do you bother with it?" he questioned.

"The stuff is cool to look at. I'd like to learn it someday."

"Stick with Western riding," he advised. "I can't picture you being all fancy."

"Mmm, maybe," she grunted.

Taylor had taken Western-style riding lessons starting when she was ten, down at Westheimer's barn, a small operation consisting of five box stalls full of scruffy, aged horses. The owner, Ralph Westheimer, a rangy cowboy in his fifties, had taught her the basics of riding.

He didn't usually say much more than "Heels down" or "Back straight" as he stood in the center of the corral and observed her endless circles.

Still, by the time she was twelve, she could walk, jog, lope, and gallop. Well, to be honest, she'd galloped only once, when the bay gelding she'd been on had been spooked by the blowing branches in the woods next to the corral and she'd nearly lost control of him.

Taylor had continued to take lessons at Ralph's place until the middle of last July. Then her mother had said she needed to stop. The lessons cost too much.

Turning the page to see even more helmets in the section, Taylor studied a photo of a girl who looked about thirteen, her own age. She was wearing one of the helmets and jumping a gorgeous chestnut horse. How graceful and elegant she looked! On Taylor's list of Things I Really Want to Do Someday was to jump a horse — and you only jumped in English-style riding.

Taylor knew it wouldn't be hard to find a place to take English riding lessons. Pheasant Valley was most definitely horse country. It was dotted with stables, horse barns, and ranches that boarded horses, gave lessons, and offered trail rides. They ranged from no-frills places such as Westheimer's to spectacular spreads like the one owned by Mrs. Ross. At the moment, the bus was winding down the incredibly curving road that bordered the lavish Ross River Ranch.

On the right they passed a fenced pasture with a red barn where two brown geldings tranquilly browsed the grass. Closer to the road, a dappled gray mare with a dark gray mane and tail grazed beside her frisky baby, who was black with three white socks. With her fingers pressed longingly on the bus window, Taylor sighed at the calm, majestic strength of the mother and the delicate spirited-ness of her long-legged baby. "Aren't they beautiful?" she remarked.

"I thought you wanted a *black* horse," her friend reminded her.

"A black Arabian is my perfect dream horse," she agreed. She'd fallen in love with the idea ever since reading *The Black Stallion* in the fifth grade. "But all horses are so gorgeous. I heard that Mrs. Ross rides a Thoroughbred for dressage, and even competes."

Taylor had never met Mrs. Ross, but she'd seen her gliding regally out of her sporty BMW, a very thin woman in her late fifties or early sixties, black hair pulled back in a sleek bun as if she were a ballerina. Devon Ross was said to be one of the wealthiest women in town, maybe the whole area.

"What's a Thoroughbred?" Travis asked.

"It's a very fancy horse breed."

"What's dressage?" Travis inquired with an edge in his voice. The suspicion in his tone reminded Taylor of the time in the third grade during a unit on France when he'd asked their teacher, "What is *escargot*, anyway?" When told it was cooked snails, he'd turned to Taylor and held his nose while he pointed his finger down his throat.

"Dressage is sort of like dancing ballet on horseback," she explained.

Travis threw his head back and laughed. "Do the horses wear tutus?"

Taylor pushed his arm. "You know they don't!"

He continued to chuckle with amusement. "Wouldn't it be funny if they did?"

"No! Dressage is really cool. I've seen it on TV, on one of those cable sports channels. There was this gorgeous horse standing on two legs and turning in a circle. I thought the rider was going to slide down his back, but somehow she stayed on. I can't imagine doing that."

Taylor's stop was in view, so she grabbed her hoodie and backpack. She was about to ask Travis if he wanted to take a bike ride with her later, but then she remembered her Egyptian report. The trip was probably better put off for another day. "See ya," she said, and hurried to the front of the bus with two sixth-graders and a seventh-grader.

Two cars, each with a waiting parent, were parked on the country road. "Ride, Taylor?" Mrs. Drew offered, sliding down her window, as she did every day.

"No, thanks. I'm fine," Taylor declined. She'd accept a ride if it was raining or snowing or frigidly cold. But otherwise she liked to maintain her independence and act as if she preferred to walk home. It didn't appeal to her to be thought of as needy. Her mother had picked her up at the stop for years, but these days she was so busy getting her new catering business going that it was impossible. Besides, it wasn't that far from the stop to her house.

The cars pulled away, and Taylor squinted into the afternoon sun. She pulled her brimmed PV softball team cap from her pack and tugged it on to shield her from the glare. After working her ponytail through the back opening, she began to walk the steep hill toward home.

Pheasant Valley had been a summer resort town from the 1900s through the 1940s. It was dotted with lakes, forests, and open fields that made it a great vacation spot. In the mid '40s people started moving into the summer cottages, which they winterized by adding heat and insulation. Most of those houses were small and clustered close together. Bigger, year-round homes were soon built on two-acre plots. Pheasant Valley was mostly countryside interspersed with these older, close-together communities and the somewhat newer two-acre developments.

Taylor's house was at the back of one of the modern housing tracts, but it was not the same as the other split-ranch-style houses. Built in 1821, it had once been the only house on the hill, and it still had the original hand-sawed beams holding up the ceiling. Taylor loved that her old former farmhouse — one of the first in Pheasant Valley — was unique among the houses in the town, even though it wasn't as fancy or big as some of them.

Near the midpoint of the winding road, a beat-up blue Ford Caravan rattled toward her from the direction of her house. She recognized the noisy van instantly.

Her mother's close friend, Claire, a petite woman in her forties with short brown hair and large brown eyes, pulled up beside Taylor and rolled down the window. From the backseat, Claire's brindle-coated pit bull, Bunny, barked a greeting.

"Taylor, hi! I was just at your house looking for you. I need you to come with me," Claire said. "You're the only one around right now who knows anything about horses."

Chapter 3

Without a second thought, Taylor hopped into the van, accustomed to its ever-present odor of wildlife. When Claire said, "Come on, I need your help," Taylor always dropped everything and went, often despite her mother's halfhearted protests.

"Where's the rescue?" Taylor asked, knowing from experience that they were headed out to help some injured or abandoned animal.

"North Somerville," Claire reported, continuing down the hill Taylor had just climbed. "I got a call from the ASPCA about a horse and pony abandoned in a barn."

"Are you kidding?" Taylor cried, horrified by the idea. "Who would do that?"

"It was a neighbor who called them," Claire revealed. "She said something about the couple being divorced and both of them driving off without taking the horse and pony with them. It seems there hasn't been anyone around in over a week, and the neighbor was pretty sure the animals were still in the barn."

"Why didn't she go look for herself?"

Claire shrugged. "At least she called."

In a little under a half hour of driving, the woodsy landscape dotted with horse pastures gave way to rolling hills of beautifully manicured lawns in front of impressive mini mansions. Claire turned the van up a long drive at the address she'd scrawled on the back of an envelope.

"Wow!" Taylor breathed, mouth agape, amazed by the grandeur of the huge brick home they were approaching. "Somebody really lives here?"

"I know. Can you imagine?" Claire agreed.

At the house, Claire rang the bell. When no one answered after several minutes, Taylor followed her across several yards of slightly overgrown grass to a cedar-shingled outbuilding. "This looks more like a big storage shed than a barn," Taylor observed.

"Let's take a look," Claire suggested, cautiously pushing open the building's door.

As Taylor stepped in behind Claire, she was suddenly plunged into complete darkness. Flailing blindly, she found Claire's wrist and wrapped her fingers around it. "Do you see them?" she asked softly.

The next second, hot breath poured down Taylor's neck. Crying out in fear, she leaped away. Horse hooves pounded the ground beside her, and an angry neighing exploded into the blackness.

Throwing the door open wide, Claire let enough sunlight pour into the building to reveal the powerful form of a black gelding. Ears flattened defensively, he snorted at them and stomped the ground, black eyes blazing.

Once her pounding heart slowed back to normal, Taylor became aware that she was detecting the heavy, acrid odor of urine. The pungent smell of a horse badly in need of grooming was also unmistakable. Horse droppings were everywhere.

His head lowered, the black horse kicked the back of the building with his rear legs, making Taylor flinch.

"When was this guy last fed?" Claire wondered aloud.

19

They scanned the area for any sign of feed or hay and spied nothing. Taylor realized that she could make out the lines of the horse's ribs.

"I brought a bag of oats. Will you be okay here while I run to the van for them?" Claire asked.

"Uh-huh," Taylor confirmed, keeping her eyes on the gelding.

Claire left and Taylor stood in the half-light of the building, taking her surroundings in with increasing clarity as her eyes adjusted. It was a simple arrangement, with two stalls on the right and room to tack up on the left. The black horse was out of his stall and standing in the open section.

Something nickered in the far stall, reminding Taylor that Claire had mentioned there was also supposed to be a pony. Taylor couldn't see one behind the half wall that separated the stalls. It had to be small and standing all the way in the back.

Cautiously keeping her back to the stalls and her eyes on the threatening black horse, Taylor sidestepped her way to the far stall. Inside was a cream-colored pony mare with a wild, frizzy blond mane of coarse hair. Standing about forty inches tall, she cowered in the corner, staring back fearfully. Her short, muscular body was turned so that she presented her rear to Taylor, her tail swishing. Taylor got the message — *Come any closer and I'll kick.*

The black horse stomped and snorted again, pawing the ground.

What were they so afraid of? Had someone mistreated them so badly? Abandoning them in here was bad enough. Both creatures were filthy and clearly malnourished. Had something even worse been done to them?

But why were they so afraid of *her*?

Taylor remembered that at Ralph's stable there had been an Appaloosa mare that went wild whenever she saw a cowboy hat because her owner before Ralph had been a cruel, cowboy hat–wearing trainer. Was it possible these two were mistaking her for someone they feared? Maybe the person who'd hurt these creatures had worn a baseball hat.

Acting on that hunch, Taylor whipped her baseball cap from her head, stuffing it into the back pocket of her jeans. To make her point clearer, she yanked out the elastic of her ponytail, letting her long hair fall free.

The black horse stared at her.

Taylor let her shoulders drop and tried not to look threatening, the way she did with the rescued dogs at Claire's house. She didn't make direct eye contact and turned away slightly.

The horse's ears slowly moved forward, changing their defensive, agitated position to one of cautious interest.

Behind her, the clatter of hooves made Taylor look over her shoulder. The pony was turning forward. Her wide-set brown eyes softened.

"Hey, pretty girl," Taylor crooned, moving slowly toward the pony.

The pony backed up two steps.

"I won't hurt you. We're here to help." Cautiously, she reached forward to stroke the pony's thick forelock. The pony allowed it, even dipping her small head slightly to allow Taylor greater access.

With a glance backward, Taylor checked on the black horse. His ears were now fully forward, and he tilted his head with curiosity.

Content that the horse was no longer threatening, Taylor turned her back to him entirely and continued to pet the small pony. "That's a good girl," she murmured. "Everything's all right now."

Taylor suddenly yelped with surprise as her head was tugged backward. Turning sharply, she was face to face with the black horse — and he was nibbling on her hair!

Chapter 4

Claire clicked off her cell phone and turned to Taylor. "Good thing I helped Ralph Westheimer round up those chickens someone let loose inside his corral. Now he owes me a favor, so he's sending over one of his stable hands with a horse trailer."

"Why would someone put chickens in his corral?" Taylor asked.

Claire smiled and shrugged. "Probably didn't want them anymore and dumped them at Ralph's during the night."

Taylor remembered being in line at the post office when a man picked up a vented box of live chickens. They made an awful racket. "I decided to try raising chickens," the man told everyone in the post office.

"I'm just glad they're not bees," said Tom, the postal clerk. "I hate when folks order bees through the mail."

This might have seemed strange somewhere else. But Pheasant Valley was an odd mix of country people, whose families had lived there for years, and newcomers, who commuted more than an hour to New York City every day to work.

Taylor looked over at the black horse and cream pony, now grazing peacefully near the outbuilding. The sunshine highlighted how filthy they both were. "They must be happy to finally be outside," Taylor commented.

"I'll bet," Claire agreed.

Taylor could see the horse and pony better in the sunlight. The horse was big, with a short head, a long neck set low on broad shoulders, and a wide chest. His ribs showed, and his coat, tail, and mane were caked with dirt. "I'm pretty sure he's a quarter horse," Taylor remarked. "When I took lessons from Ralph, that's the kind of horse he mostly had. You can tell from the long neck and wide chest. They're great horses."

"Why do they call them quarter?" Claire asked.

"Because when you race one, it can run really fast for a quarter of a mile." Taylor remembered Ralph telling her that during a lesson once.

Claire's eyes lit with a plan. "Maybe Ralph will keep these guys, at least for a while."

"Are we allowed to just *take* someone else's horse and pony?" Taylor questioned.

"We can because back at the van I called the ASPCA and had the folks there call the sheriff. The sheriff is trying to locate one of the owners to get permission."

"What if they won't give permission?" Taylor asked.

"Then they could be charged with animal neglect and abuse," Claire said as she took her cell phone back out of her pocket. "That's how it's worked with other animal rescues I've done, anyway," she added. "I've never actually done a horse rescue before."

"I know," Taylor said, remembering the many times she'd gone out with Claire. They'd come back with lots of dogs and cats, several abandoned domestic bunnies, and even a broken-winged goose. Once, they'd even brought back a baby crocodile — but never a horse and pony.

"I'm going to call him right now and find out if he's been able to contact the owners," Claire said, punching the sheriff's number into her phone.

While Claire called, Taylor made her way toward the animals. The horse lifted his head, interested, and stepped toward her. The little pony moved at the same time.

Taylor made a soft clicking sound, inviting the horse to join her. He neighed in response but stayed where he was.

Patting her jeans pockets, she hoped she had a Life Saver or a wrapped peppermint to offer, but she came up empty. Not far from the outbuilding stood a low tree that Taylor realized was full of small crab apples. The horses at Ralph's loved it when she brought them apples.

Taylor ran to the tree and shook the lowest branch she could reach. A shower of small green and red apples fell around her. Shielding herself with a raised arm, she laughed and jumped out of the way. When the down-pour of fruit stopped she stuffed several of the apples into the pockets of her hooded sweatshirt and hurried across the yard.

Taylor wasn't even halfway to them when the black horse caught the sweet fragrance of the apples. He lifted his head high and began to walk quickly toward Taylor. The little pony trailed him.

Before Taylor could even reach into her front pocket, the horse was nuzzling her belly, trying to get at the treats. Taylor laughed and pushed his muzzle away from her pocket. "Like apples a little, do you?" she joked, taking one from her pocket.

Holding her palm flat, she presented one to him. Taylor had learned — the hard way — that when presenting a horse with food, a flat palm helped keep her fingers from being accidentally nipped. The black horse chomped the apple in half with one bite. The other half tumbled to his feet. In an instant it, too, was in his mouth. He was about to dive into her pocket for more, but Taylor stepped away from him. "Hold on, greedy. What about your friend here?" she said with a grin.

Taylor moved to the pony and presented a small apple. The pony knocked it to the ground with her muzzle and then ate it.

Hot breath warmed Taylor's cheek, and in the next instant she received a soft but insistent nudge on her shoulder. "Okay, okay," she said, chuckling again and turning toward the horse behind her. "Hold your . . . horses."

Claire walked over, smiling at them. "I see you've made friends," she commented.

"I don't know if they like me, but they *love* my apples," Taylor replied as she fed another largish one to the horse.

"The sheriff can't locate the owners, but he's authorized us to take them out of here," Claire reported. As she spoke, a flatbed truck hauling a horse trailer pulled up the drive by the house. "Here's Ralph's ranch hand with the trailer."

"I didn't see any rope or halters or anything in that shed," Taylor recalled.

"Go check again while I run up and talk to the driver," Claire suggested. "He might have something."

Taylor jogged back to the shed and stepped inside. Now that it had aired for a while the building wasn't quite as pungent as earlier, but it caused Taylor to sneeze and cough just the same. On a dusty shelf in the tack area she searched for a halter or two that they could attach a rope to and lead the animals to the trailer, but she found only a short piece of frayed rope and an empty feed bag. Scanning the walls for anything that might be hung up, her eyes fell on wooden nameplates next to the stalls. She hadn't noticed them before.

She crossed to them and read: ALBERT — AMERICAN QUARTER HORSE. Taylor was pleased to have been correct in identifying his breed. The other plate read: PIXIE — SHETLAND PONY.

When Taylor stepped outside once more, Albert and Pixie were waiting for her right by the door. Albert again probed her pocket in search of fruit. Taylor laughed lightly. "You apple hogs," she teased them.

Taylor took an apple from her pocket and was about to extend the fruit to Albert when an idea came to her. Still holding the apple, she stepped backward four steps. Albert moved forward and Pixie followed him. Taylor realized that Pixie followed Albert everywhere.

Taylor kept going, stepping backward, until she was nearly to the house with the two animals trailing after her. "Well, look at that," Claire said admiringly. "Aren't you the clever one?"

Claire stood beside Ralph's stable hand, a tall blond guy in overalls named Rick. Taylor knew him a little from riding at Ralph's place. Claire and Rick had been walking back to the shed but were still closer to the trailer in the driveway. "Lead those two right on into that open trailer," Claire said to Taylor.

Rick was carrying halters and lead lines. "Wow! Are those guys ever dirty!" he said when he saw the animals. "And they look starved."

"I bet they'll clean up nice," Taylor said, already feeling a need to stick up for the two animals that had fallen into her care. She offered Albert and Pixie the apples they'd been after.

"Maybe," Rick agreed in a doubtful tone. "Good luck finding a new home for them, though. I don't know anybody who'd want two raggedy characters like them."

"They just need a good grooming," Taylor insisted, surprised by how defensive she felt.

Rick raised his brows skeptically. "If you say so. Anyway, let's halter them in case I need to tie them in for the ride."

Albert once again began sticking his muzzle into Taylor's pocket. "Don't give them many more of those," Claire advised. "We don't know how their bellies will handle the trip, if you know what I mean."

Rick approached Albert with the halter. Albert neighed at him aggressively, angrily. He stomped the ground with his right hoof. Pixie whinnied shrilly, turning her back on Rick, ready to kick.

Taylor recalled their first encounter in the shed. "I don't think they like men very much," she advised Rick.

"I guess not," Rick agreed. He turned toward Claire and offered the halter to her.

Claire waved it away. "I've never done that before. Taylor, would you be able to halter them?"

Taylor was suddenly nervous, not sure how the horse would react. At Ralph Westheimer's place she'd learned not only how to ride a horse but also the basics of grooming and tacking — under the guidance of Ralph's watchful eye.

"I've never done it completely on my own," Taylor admitted, reaching out to take the halter from Rick, "but I'll give it a try."

After all, she thought, *what could happen — other than being kicked, bitten, or stepped on?*

Taylor held the halter at Albert's eye level. "It's just a halter, boy. You've seen this before." She was talking to soothe Albert but also to calm her own fears.

With a soft whinny, Albert ducked his head down toward Taylor.

Taylor smiled softly. He was making it easy. Albert's cooperation, this sign of friendship, melted her anxieties. She reached forward and with one hand stroked the area between Albert's ears called the crown. With her other hand she slipped the leather halter over Albert's ears, gently moving the halter over his muzzle. He readily accepted the halter as though he'd done this a thousand times.

Then she did the same to Pixie. Attaching Rick's lead lines to the halters, she led them easily up the ramp and into the trailer. "It won't be a long ride," she told them as she left. "You'll be okay."

"They seem okay. I don't think you have to tie them in," she told Rick.

When the trailer was closed and latched, Claire turned to Rick. "So, I guess we should meet you back at Ralph's stable," she said to him.

But Rick shook his head. "Ralph said he can't take them. He's full up."

"Not even outside?" Claire pressed.

"He just bought three new horses at auction last weekend, and he's got them corralled outside," Rick said. "Plus he's boarding two new horses this week, and he's hoping to get even more soon. Times are tough, and the number of kids taking lessons is down, so he *really* depends on boarding."

Claire sighed, and her brows knit into a perplexed expression.

"Where else can we take them?" Taylor asked.

"That's a good question," Claire replied.

Chapter 5

"**A**re you sure this is where you want to put them?" Rick asked, a dubious expression playing across his face. Taylor, Rick, and Claire were in Claire's driveway, standing beside the horse trailer. "I don't think you're allowed to keep a horse in your front yard."

The three of them turned their attention to the yard, which was circumscribed by a split-rail fence wrapped in chicken-wire net fencing. Bunny the pit bull had hopped out of Claire's van and was now racing around the outside of the fence, while inside, six rescued dogs of different breeds and sizes barked playfully and chased her. "Pipe down," Claire told them firmly. At the sound of her command, they all quieted. "I try to keep the barking to a minimum for the neighbors," she explained to Rick and Taylor.

Pheasant Valley was full of farms, ranches, and private homes with sprawling acreage. But Claire's small house was one of the older, smaller, former summer cottages, close to Mohegan Lake. It was in a community of old vacation houses situated close together. The only open space was a field across the street that led to a wood behind it.

Even though she had enclosed her property, Claire was constantly at odds with certain neighbors who objected to her ever-changing menagerie, especially when it got too raucous. "This isn't enough room, and you have a lot of other animals," Rick remarked, looking at the eighth of an acre yard doubtfully.

"It's as big as a small corral, and horses like to be with other animals. They're herd animals and don't like to be lonely," Taylor commented, remembering that Ralph never liked to corral a horse by itself.

Claire laughed. "They definitely would *not* be lonely here."

"Maybe you'd better have the sheriff find them a place," Rick suggested.

"No!" Taylor objected. "They've already been locked up for too long."

"He wouldn't put them in jail," Rick replied.

"But they might wind up in some horse pound somewhere," Taylor argued. She wasn't sure there even was such a thing as a horse pound, but she didn't want to take a chance on it.

"We'll only keep them here temporarily," Claire said, "until I can find someone to take them."

"Who would want them?" Rick asked.

"I would," Taylor said quickly.

"Why?" Rick asked her. "They both need a lot of work. They might never be any good to anybody."

"Sure they will be," Claire said, walking around to the back of the trailer and unlatching it. "We'll get them all fixed up. Won't we, Taylor?"

"No problem," Taylor replied, not exactly sure how they were going to do this but liking Claire's positive attitude.

Claire entered the trailer and Albert danced nervously. "You'd better get them out, Taylor," Claire called. "It seems this horse only wants you."

Taylor was surprised at the small skip of joy and pride

her heart did when she heard Claire's words. Albert liked her best. It was probably silly to even care, but just the same, a smile came to her lips as she entered the trailer and saw how he settled down right away.

Taylor unloaded Albert and Pixie without any trouble. All she had to do was lead Albert down the ramp. Pixie came right behind them without even being summoned.

Rick unlatched the gate to the yard for Taylor. When Albert saw him there, he came to an abrupt stop. "Maybe you should move from the gate," Taylor suggested to Rick.

As soon as Rick stepped away, Albert moved forward, bringing Pixie with him into the yard. Excited by their new boarders, Bunny darted into the yard and ran protective circles around Albert and Pixie, keeping the other curious dogs back. "Good girl, Bunny," Claire praised her pet. "Let them get settled before they make friends with the other animals."

Looking skyward, Taylor was a little startled that it was already very dusky. After the long, fun-filled days of summer she was always a little sad to see the sunlight gradually shorten as the season ended at the start of school.

"It looks like it might rain," Claire commented, following Taylor's upward gaze.

"That's good. I thought it was dark because the days were getting shorter."

"Well, they are, a little, but I think there are also storm clouds rolling in," Claire said. "What are we going to do with these guys if it starts to pour?"

"Could you build them a lean-to?" Rick suggested from the driveway side of the fence. "They'd probably be happier with some kind of shelter. They're not used to being in the wild."

Claire's eyes darted around the yard, scanning for building materials.

Distant thunder clapped the sky. Albert neighed nervously, shifting his weight from foot to foot. Pixie's anxious eyes fixed on Albert. Taylor recalled a show she'd seen on TV. It was about wild horse herds and how they often got hit by lightning because they were in open pastures. She wondered if, because of this, all horses feared thunderstorms; or maybe they were simply scared of the noise and furious light.

"I guess we'd better get started right away," Claire said. "We don't want the big guy getting so spooked that he leaps the fence and runs down the street."

Taylor imagined an awful scene of a terrified Albert

in the street among screeching cars. It made her shudder. "I'll tie their lines to the fence," she said.

Albert's eyes had a wild look in them that worried Taylor. He snorted unhappily. Pixie seemed calmer, but she was still watching Albert, taking her cues from him.

Taylor placed her hand on Albert's neck. She could feel his heart pumping hard and realized she must be somewhere near his jugular vein. "It's okay. It's okay," she soothed. "Really. Nothing's going to hurt you. It's just a storm."

Taylor took Albert's lead line and led him to the fence. She was confident Pixie would follow, and the pony did. Taylor quickly tied them to the fence using the hitch knots she'd learned at Ralph's place.

"I have some planks in the garage," Claire said. "I'm thinking we can make some kind of three-sided shelter if we attach it to the house I have for the feral cats."

Taylor glanced at the feral cat shed. It had two levels and was about seven feet high. It would probably be the right height for Albert if they built the shelter to the height of the shed.

"Rick, could you help us?" Claire requested.

"I'd like to help you," Rick replied. "But I've got to get

this trailer back to Ralph. He needs it to transport one of the new horses. He said you can keep his tack stuff as long as you need it, though."

"Okay, thanks," Claire told him with a parting wave. She walked over beside Taylor. "We'd better get busy building this thing. It's just you and me, kiddo, and this storm is coming in fast."

A raindrop rolled down Taylor's nose, and she caught it on her tongue. With one hand she steadied a plank she had been nailing to the cat shed. With the other, she searched in her hoodie pocket for nails but didn't find any more.

When the rain had started, Claire had quickly herded all her dogs into the house. Those that wouldn't go in found shelter on her porch, which was open but covered with an awning. Now Claire was in the garage searching for supplies.

"I need more nails," Taylor shouted through the driving rain as Claire came out of her garage with a very large blue tarp. Taylor realized the tarp was the winter cover to Claire's aboveground pool.

"Hold on! I'll bring them to you," Claire called, turning back inside the garage.

While she waited, Taylor checked to see how Albert and Pixie were faring in the downpour that had come upon them so quickly. Albert was clearly on high alert. His ears swiveled in every direction as he studied his new surroundings. Pixie stayed close to Albert's flank, her head down.

When lightning flashed in the sky, though, Albert's ears flattened, and he neighed shrilly. Pixie dug her sturdy rear legs into the dirt, almost as if preparing to kick any approaching lightning back up into the clouds.

Claire emerged from the garage with a coffee can of nails. She and Taylor finished securing the planks to the shed and then threw the tarp on top.

Taylor was nailing down her side of the tarp when she heard a car engine coming up the driveway, windshield wipers slapping. Climbing up two steps on her freestanding ladder, she peered over the top and saw her mother getting out of their car.

Taylor's mother, Jennifer Henry, was dressed for the rain in a yellow hooded slicker and high blue rubber boots. From under her hood, a few of her blonde curls

44

blew in the wind as she pulled the gate open and stepped into the yard.

Taylor had texted her mother, saying she was on a rescue with Claire, but that was all she'd said about it. It didn't take Taylor's mother long to figure out the rest, though.

Chapter 6

Taylor's mother saw Pixie and Albert standing in the rain and jumped back, startled. "You rescued *them*?" Jennifer cried, looking at Taylor and Claire, wide-eyed with surprise. "You can't keep a horse and pony in your yard, can you? Why are they here?"

"Tell you later," Claire shouted to her over the rain and wind. "There are some old white towels in the garage. Would you bring them out here? Try to keep them dry."

Taylor's mom ran into the garage and came out with a stack of towels with a black garbage bag draped on top. She ducked below the tarp stretched above the two sets of planks. "Is this your pool cover?" she asked.

"Yep," Claire replied with a laugh. "Just put the towels on top of the garbage bag in a corner for now."

"You can't keep a horse and pony here," Jennifer repeated. Then a blast of laughter came from her lips. "Why am I even bothering to tell you that, Claire? I should know by now that you do things your own way."

"Exactly," Claire said with a smile. "So pick up a hammer and help us finish this. Then I'll make you a cup of tea and tell you all about it when we're done."

Claire and her mother had gone inside, but Taylor stayed with the horse and pony. Standing in the newly constructed lean-to shelter with Albert and Pixie, she looked down at the once-white towel in her hands. "Wow! Were you ever *dirty!*" Taylor told Albert. She'd been toweling him dry for close to fifteen minutes and had already saturated three towels with mud. His time in the rain had already washed a great deal of the dirt from him.

All Taylor really wanted to do was get the two of them dry so they wouldn't catch a chill. She'd worry about cleaning them once the weather was nicer. At least the rain had helped.

Outside the shelter, the rain had subsided into a drizzle. A fold in the tarp created a downspout that sent a rivulet of water pouring steadily in the right corner of the makeshift shelter. Albert and Pixie positioned themselves near it and delighted in drinking from the puddle it created in the grass.

Taylor picked up a fourth towel and swept along Albert's right flank. His ribs protruded from his side, and she quivered slightly as a blast of white-hot anger shot through her. How coldhearted could a person be to neglect these sweet animals like this? It was inexcusable! Infuriating!

And then a sad tenderness swept away the rage and almost overwhelmed her. "You don't have to worry anymore," Taylor told them softly, blinking wetness from her lashes. "We've got you now. It's all going to be good from here on out."

Taylor heard the gate creak open, and in the next moment Travis stepped into the doorway of the shelter. "I don't believe it!" he cried as he stepped inside. "Is this cool or what?!"

She had texted him to come as fast as he could to Claire's house, saying only that she had something

amazing to show him. He'd replied: RLLY? IN MDDLE
OF AWSM NEW BTMAN.

Annoyed, Taylor hadn't even bothered to respond.
She wished she could share Travis's intense love of comics
but she just didn't see the point, at least not to the degree
of obsession Travis brought to it. Sometimes it seemed as
though he loved his comics and superheroes more than
anything else in the world.

But there Travis was.

All Taylor's anger and sadness evaporated at the sight
of her friend, and a wide grin spread across her face. "I
know! I know! Aren't they great?"

Albert neighed loudly at Travis.

Travis jumped back so suddenly that he fell on his butt
in the wet grass.

Taylor didn't mean to laugh, but it was too funny, and
she could see he wasn't hurt. "Oh, sorry. I forgot to tell
you — they don't like men."

Travis stood and brushed wet grass from the back of
his jeans. "Oh, thanks for telling me *now*. I should be glad
he didn't bite me."

"Relax, you're all right," she said.

"Did you get these in a rescue?" he asked from outside the shelter.

"Uh-huh."

"Are they yours to keep?"

How she longed to say yes! "No. I guess Claire will find them a home."

"You should keep them," Travis insisted. "He's a black horse just like you've always wanted. Is he an Arabian?"

Taylor shook her head. "Quarter horse."

"Close enough," Travis said, unconcerned. "Ask your mother if you can keep him, at least."

"I couldn't separate them. This pony loves Albert like crazy. She follows him everywhere."

"Then take them both."

"I couldn't. Where would I put them?" Taylor questioned.

"In your yard," Travis said, as if the answer should have been obvious.

Taylor shook her head again. "It's not nearly big enough."

Travis spread his arms and gestured widely. "Neither is this yard, but here they are."

"This is only temporary until Claire finds a better place for them."

"Imagine if you got a horse before Plum Mason did! That would make her really crazy!" Travis said with a mischievous grin.

"I thought you didn't care about stuff like that," Taylor commented.

"I don't. I'm just saying. I'd love to see her face."

"It might be funny to see Plum get all mad, but that isn't why I'd want to keep them." Taylor cast a longing glance at Albert and Pixie. "They're just so sweet and beautiful. And they've been treated so badly. I'd take great care of them."

Albert stuck his head under some rainwater falling from the top of the tarp. Sputtering, he shook his forelock and mane, spraying them all.

Taylor jumped away, laughing. "Like I'm not already wet enough, Albert!" she joked, flinging the water from her hands at him.

Albert sputtered, nodded his head, and licked his lips. Taylor was sure he was playing along. Pixie neighed cheerfully.

Oh, if she only *could* keep them! Taylor felt the desire to own them as an ache deep inside.

Was it *really* impossible?

Of course it was!

But it would be so wonderful!

What would it hurt to at least ask?

Taylor and her mother had just finished supper and were still sitting at the table in their kitchen. After leaving Claire's place, they'd returned home, showered, and pulled on sweats. Jennifer had thrown last night's leftover chicken into some cream of mushroom soup and served it over rice. It felt cozy to be dry and warm and fed. "Any dessert?" Taylor asked.

"I had extra brownies left today," Jennifer replied.

Taylor's face lit with pleasure. "Awesome!"

Jennifer got up to get them out of a large canvas tote in a corner of the kitchen. "It would have been more awesome if I had sold them all," she remarked.

Ever since Taylor's mother and father split up a few months ago, money had become much tighter. Her father,

Steve, had moved across town, and he didn't come visit her regularly. Taylor had the feeling that maybe he didn't pay his child support all that regularly, either, although her mother never complained about it directly. What she said was, "I have to be more careful with money these days. You understand, don't you?"

To make extra money besides what she earned as a waitress at the Pheasant Valley Diner, she'd begun making desserts and selling them to the local delis, supermarkets, and restaurants. People began asking Jennifer to supply food for their private parties and local events. Now Taylor's mother was working long hours to get her small catering business, Jennifer's Cooking, going while still keeping her waitress job.

"I booked another job today," she reported as she handed Taylor a brownie square. "The Pheasant Valley PTA luncheon."

"All right, Mom!" Taylor cheered. "Don't make the food too good, though. Some of those teachers don't deserve it."

"Like who?" Jennifer asked, sitting at the table and nibbling on her brownie.

"Remember Mrs. Kirchner from when I was in the third grade? She was evil."

Jennifer laughed. "She was not! What was evil about her?"

"Everything! She had the meanest expression. All us kids would shake when she came into the room."

Jennifer chuckled. "You exaggerate!"

"No, I mean it. She was awful."

"Isn't she Claire's neighbor?"

Taylor nodded. "I dive into the bushes to hide when I see her over there."

"You do not!" Jennifer said with a grin of amusement.

"Maybe not the bushes," Taylor allowed, "but I definitely hide."

"Mrs. Kirchner has taught at the elementary school since I was there," Jennifer recalled. "Come to think of it, Claire and I used to hide from her, too."

"Told you!"

Jennifer got up and began clearing the supper plates, stacking them in the dishwasher. Taylor helped. "Mom, is there any way I could work with you in the catering business?"

"I don't know," her mother replied. "It's nice of you to offer, though."

"Well, not really as nice as you think. I'm looking for a way to earn extra money."

"Oh, I see," Jennifer said as she rinsed a pot. "You'd want to be paid."

"Not a lot," Taylor clarified quickly. She could see that she'd disappointed her mother, who'd assumed she was simply offering to lend a hand. Taylor was certainly willing to help out. It was just that this plan might benefit both of them.

"And what do you need this extra money for?" Jennifer asked.

Taylor's throat suddenly felt dry. She swallowed hard. "Well, I was thinking . . . It wasn't really my idea, but Travis suggested it and it makes sense, in a way. I know you won't like the idea at first, but just think about it before you answer."

"What?" Jennifer asked, her voice rising slightly with impatience.

"Promise you'll think about it before you say no?"

"Just say it!"

Taylor coughed to clear her throat. Then she began

talking even more rapidly, afraid that if she didn't race through her speech, she'd lose her nerve. "Here's the thing. Albert and Pixie are really, really great. And they love each other so much. I don't think Pixie could even live without Albert. A chance like this to get a horse and pony for free will probably never, ever come again. So . . . you see?"

Jennifer stared blankly at Taylor. "I'm afraid I don't see," she admitted after a moment. "Who's getting them for free?"

Taylor steeled her nerves, but her reply came out in croak. "Me?"

"What?" her mother asked again, her voice thick with incredulous disbelief.

This was Taylor's moment to be persuasive. It was now or never and she knew it. "I could build a split-rail fence, like Claire has, in the back. And then I could work with you after school and you would pay me so I could buy them oats and hay and —"

"Wait a minute!" Jennifer cut her off. "You want to keep those two animals in *our* backyard?"

"I know it's not really big enough, but it's got room for them to walk around, and then when I've earned enough money —"

"No! Absolutely not! What are you thinking, Taylor? Have you lost it completely?" Jennifer shook her head and sighed heavily. "How can you even ask that?"

Not knowing what else to do, Taylor resorted to an old childhood standby. "Pleeaaassse," she begged. "I love them."

"You just met them this afternoon."

"But it was love at first sight! Albert's almost exactly like the horse I've been dreaming about all my life, so it's as if I've known him forever. And Pixie goes where Albert goes, so I have to have them both."

Jennifer sat down again at the table. Taylor didn't like the weary expression on her face. "Taylor, I'm working day and night just to pay the bills. We can't take on a horse, let alone a horse *and* a pony. It's out of the question."

Taylor knew her mother was right. What she was asking was unreasonable and even insensitive. Her mother worked so hard. Taylor couldn't help being disappointed, though, deeply disappointed.

And then another emotion rose within her and overtook the disappointment. The feeling took her by surprise, but she felt no desire to control it.

Taylor was seized by a strong, deep anger.

"Can't you think about what *I* want?" she demanded, standing.

"Taylor!"

"I mean it! I'm always saying I understand why I can't have stuff. And I do understand. But I want Albert and Pixie more than I've ever wanted anything in my life!" she shouted.

With hot tears of fury brimming in her eyes, Taylor stormed out the kitchen door, letting it slam behind her.

She got as far as the garage before she stopped and let the tears spill freely, once again feeling the full weight of her disappointment.

Chapter 7

On Saturday, Taylor was up by seven. She shoveled down a bowl of Cheerios, got on her bike, and headed for Claire's. It had rained off and on through the night, but the morning sky was a clear blue. The leaves and puddles in the road glistened with leftover wetness. It wasn't really cold, though the first invigorating snap of fall weather was unmistakable.

Taylor lived in the bowl of the valley, while Claire's house was on the rim. That made for tough, uphill pedaling along winding Mohegan Lake Road, named for the Native Americans who had once lived in Pheasant Valley.

When she arrived at Claire's, the rescued dogs were asleep under the awning on the side deck. One of them noticed her and got up. He began barking, and she shushed him as she let herself in through the gate.

Before she'd left on Friday, she had covered Pixie and Albert each with a blanket. Now they stood contentedly side by side eating hay. Taylor smiled as Albert lifted his head to bring his muzzle to Pixie's. The two friends nuzzled each other a moment before returning to the pile of hay they'd been munching.

Albert noticed Taylor and nickered a welcome. She joined Pixie and Albert under the dripping tarp and petted the side of Albert's neck. Brushing her hand along his mane, she realized it was full of snarls that had snagged debris — small twigs, leaf bits, even dead flies. The rain hadn't washed him fully clean, either, but had left mud rivulets down his side.

Pixie looked just as bad, possibly worse.

Once the weather cleared, Taylor would wash them properly and comb out their manes and tails. She'd braid them and then brush their coats until they shined. With her love and care, Taylor was sure these two could be brought back to the healthy state they must have enjoyed at one time. She was determined to make it happen.

"Reality check, Taylor," she scolded herself. "They're not yours, remember?"

So what? It didn't matter. She'd clean them up, anyway. If they were going to find good homes, they would have to look presentable. If they looked good, someone was bound to want to ride them.

Taylor suddenly realized that, though she'd assumed they could be ridden, she didn't know that for sure. There hadn't been a saddle or bridle in their shed.

"Would you let me ride you, Albert?" she wondered, speaking more to herself than to Albert. Taylor had never ridden a horse bareback, but she had seen Ralph do it occasionally for short distances. He always warned her not to, saying it was much too dangerous.

"It can't be that dangerous if we're just walking in a fenced-in yard," she considered, petting Albert's side. "We'll only walk slowly."

Checking around, Taylor searched for something to stand on for a boost up. The wooden bench from the outdoor table set would do. She had a halter but no reins. That was all right. There was really no place to go, so there was no need to use the reins for direction.

Taylor dragged the picnic table bench over to his side and stood on it. She breathed deeply to steady herself. "Here I come, Albert. Please don't move, or I'm going to land right under you."

Albert swung his head around to look at her curiously.

"It's just me," Taylor spoke to him soothingly.

Albert sputtered and Taylor sensed impatience in the sound. Maybe it was her imagination; she wasn't sure. Did he want her to climb on? She hoped so. It was possible that no one had ridden him in a long time and that he missed it.

"Here goes," she said, swinging her leg and arm across his back and pitching herself forward.

"Nononono . . . nooo!" she squealed as she felt herself sliding across to his other side, taking the blanket on his back along with her. Curling her toes to stop her forward motion, she clutched at his neck, halting her momentum. "Whew. That was close," she said, imagining how painful it would have been to land headfirst on the other side.

In the next minute, Taylor had pulled herself up onto Albert's back and patted his withers and managed to straighten the blanket beneath her. "Good boy."

Clicking gently, she pressed his sides with her knees to move him. Without hesitation, he walked forward out of the homemade shelter. Taylor's head hit the top of the tarp, showering both rider and horse with a frigid spray of cold water. Albert neighed shrilly at the sudden cold but kept walking.

Pixie emerged from the lean-to. "No, Pixie, you go back," Taylor instructed with a wave of her arm.

The little pony hesitated and then kept on coming.

"I said go back," Taylor repeated as Albert walked on, but Pixie kept following. "Oh, I guess it doesn't matter," she mumbled, accepting the fact that Pixie would not be deterred from going wherever Albert went.

Taylor breathed in the misty air and smiled broadly. How great to be riding bareback right here in Claire's front yard!

Taylor rode Albert at a walk all along the circumference of the fence, with Pixie staying close behind. A car went by and the man driving stared at her with goggle-eyed amazement. The look on his face made Taylor laugh out loud.

A gray-haired woman walking a small white dog on a leash came down the road. She wore a raincoat, black rubber boots, and a sour expression. Taylor recognized her right away. It was Mrs. Kirchner, her former third-grade teacher.

Mrs. Kirchner had her eyes on the road, watching her dog. She stopped by the corner of the fence to pick up her dog's poop and bag it. When she straightened, she saw Taylor, Albert, and Pixie on the other side of the fence.

Mrs. Kirchner staggered back in shock, nearly tripping over her little dog.

Taylor clamped her teeth together to keep from laughing.

The dog started yapping fiercely at Albert and Pixie. Albert sidestepped nervously, and Taylor soothed him by stroking his neck.

"Taylor Henry! What are you doing on a horse?" Mrs. Kirchner cried, as though Taylor were back in her third-grade class and had ridden a horse into the classroom. "And what is that *little* horse doing there?"

"She's a pony," Taylor explained.

"Well, what does that matter?" the woman shouted irately. "Why are they there? Why are you riding them?"

"I just wanted to. We're not bothering anyone," Taylor

answered, not quite understanding why Mrs. Kirchner was getting so red-faced.

"Not hurting anyone!" Mrs. Kirchner cried with a shrillness that made Albert sputter. "Not hurting anyone! That's hardly the point! There are laws about this kind of thing! You can't have a horse and pony in a front yard. It's intolerable that we have to put up with the usual menagerie she houses here. But a horse! A pony!"

Claire must have heard the shouting because just then she opened her front door and stood there dressed in flannel pajamas and Crocs. Five dogs raced out around her and careened down to the fence, barking madly. Alerted by the noise, four more dogs scrambled over the porch gate to join them. They jumped up on the split-rail fence, yapping at Mrs. Kirchner and her dog.

Taylor leaned forward, preparing to grab on to Albert's mane if the dogs suddenly made him bolt or rear. Her heart raced and she breathed deeply, willing herself to remain calm. She knew a horse was sensitive to the mood of its rider.

Albert stood calmly as the dogs raced around him. Taylor realized he wasn't going to be spooked by them and relaxed.

Mrs. Kirchner scooped her dog into her arms. "This is really too much! What's next — a camel? I wouldn't put it past her!"

Claire clapped her hands sharply as she made her way toward the fence. "Stop that barking!" she commanded her dogs.

"I'm going home right now and calling the sheriff," Mrs. Kirchner threatened Claire.

"Calm down, Mrs. Kirchner. The sheriff already knows I have the horse and pony," Claire said.

"He *knows* they're in your front yard?" Mrs. Kirchner shot back skeptically.

Not exactly, Taylor thought, but she said nothing.

"We'll see just what the sheriff does and does not know," Mrs. Kirchner shouted over her shoulder as she stormed away. "If he has permitted this, he will certainly get a piece of my mind. We pay the taxes that pay his salary."

Claire exhaled with a deep, slow breath and rubbed her forehead. Taylor looked down at her. "Sorry."

"What for?" Claire asked.

"If I hadn't been riding Albert with Pixie tagging along, she might not have noticed."

68

Claire chuckled a little sadly. "She'd have noticed eventually."

"What will the sheriff do?" Taylor asked.

"Probably give me twenty-four hours to find some-place else to put these guys. If I don't, he'll give me a summons."

"What if you can't find them a home?"

Claire sighed unhappily. "He'll come with a trailer and take them."

"And then what?" Taylor asked.

"He'll try to sell them at an auction."

Taylor ran her hand along Albert's bony side. "What if nobody wants to buy them?"

Claire bent to pet Bunny, who was licking her hand. "Don't think about it, Taylor. You don't want to know."

Chapter 8

*A*fter that, it was *all* Taylor could think about. On Sunday she'd called Travis to tell him everything that had happened. "Kirchner is such an old witch," he'd sympathized.

Now, on Monday morning, she sat beside Travis on the bus and revealed the horrifying results of her Sunday-night Google search. "Horse meat. Killing horses for horse meat is illegal in the United States, but slaughterhouses in Canada and Mexico send reps to these auctions, and they take the horses back with them."

Travis scrunched his face into an expression of disgust. "Horse meat! Gross! Won't the sheriff just put them down?"

Taylor covered her face with her hands. "That's not much better!"

"Don't worry," Travis said. "Someone will want them."

"Like who?"

"I don't know. Someone."

"Who's going to want *both* of them?" Taylor wailed.

"I don't know. I guess you'll have to split them up."

Taylor put her hands down. Travis's words had caused a knot in her stomach. "No! They can't be separated. They're best friends. It would be too cruel."

"Not as cruel as . . . you know . . . the other thing," Travis said quietly.

Mrs. Kirchner had, indeed, called the sheriff's office. Because Claire had gone to high school with the deputy who came to her house, he gave her three days, instead of twenty-four hours, to find a home for Albert and Pixie.

"That's not much time," Travis commented.

"I know. This is already the second day. We have to find just the right home for them, too. It's got to be someone who really loves horses," Taylor said as the bus pulled up in front of the school. "Someone who will give them the care they need to get better. Ralph came by Claire's on

Sunday and looked at their teeth — that's how you can judge a horse's age."

"How does that work?" Travis asked.

"It's interesting," Taylor replied. She had been there on Sunday when Ralph stopped by, and he'd explained it to her. "Under age five, a horse still has what they call milk teeth. After that the teeth get more angled. By age ten, a small groove starts at the top of the incisor, and by twenty, that groove has reached the lower end of the tooth. So you can guess the age of a horse between ten and twenty depending on how long the groove is. But by the time a horse is twenty years old, the groove starts to go away at the top, so you can tell if a horse is older than that."

"Man, that's cool," Travis remarked.

"I know," Taylor agreed. "He figures that Albert is about fifteen, which is a full-grown horse. Pixie is over twenty. That would be old for a horse, but ponies live longer. Still, she's not young, and she needs someone who will treat her gently."

Taylor and Travis joined the flow of kids getting off the bus and entering the middle school's front door.

In the crowd Taylor thought she heard someone call her name. Turning, she saw Plum Mason and a few of her snooty friends — not anyone who would be calling to her.

Turning forward, she continued into the school. Suddenly, she felt a hand on her shoulder. Startled, she swung around and faced Plum. "Didn't you hear me calling you?" Plum asked, annoyed.

"What?" was all Taylor could think of to say. That Plum was calling to her was practically unthinkable. Aside from the occasional snide classroom comment — as had happened last Friday — the girl never spoke to her.

"Are you deaf or something?" Plum said. Her friends came along, forming a loose semicircle behind Plum. They snickered at Plum's remark.

"Come on, Taylor," Travis said. He'd walked nearly to the staircase but turned back when he noticed that Taylor had been waylaid by Plum and her pals. "Let's go."

Taylor made a move to walk away with Travis.

"Wait!" Plum stopped her. "I just want Claire Black's phone number. You're friends with her, right?"

Taylor narrowed her eyes suspiciously. "Why do you want it?" Claire used only a cell phone, and Taylor knew the number by heart. But she wasn't about to give it to Plum — not without a very good reason.

Plum sighed, vexed at the inconvenience of explaining herself to Taylor. "I don't think that's any of your business. So, do you know her number or not?"

"No!" Taylor blurted without a moment's hesitation.

"No?" Plum sneered doubtfully. "Then how do you get in touch with her?"

"My mother knows it. I don't."

Plum rolled her eyes. "Then could you ask your *mother* for it and tell me tomorrow?"

Travis took Taylor by the crook of her elbow and pulled her away from Plum. "If she remembers," he told Plum, "which she might not."

"What are you, her *boyfriend*?" Plum sneered.

"Why, did you want me to be *your* boyfriend?" Travis shot back.

"Ew! Like I would ever go out with you!" Plum replied.

Travis responded by contorting his face into a comical knot and crossing his eyes at Plum.

Taylor glanced at Travis's horrible face and hooted with laughter.

"Loser!" Plum snarled.

The buzzer for first period sounded, giving Taylor an excuse to move away from Plum altogether.

"Don't forget that number!" Plum called after her as she hurried down a different hallway from the one Taylor was headed for.

"You know Claire's number, don't you?" Travis remarked as they once again headed toward their class-rooms.

Taylor nodded. "Sure I do, but I'm not giving it to Plum."

"Just on principle — because she's Plum?"

"Yeah, but also . . ." A thought had come to her that was so awful she didn't even want to say it out loud.

"Also what?" Travis pressed.

Taylor stopped and stepped closer to Travis. She dropped her voice to a low, confiding tone. "What if she's heard about Albert and Pixie? What if she wants them?"

"How would she hear about them?" Travis asked.

"PV is a small town," Taylor reminded him. "Everyone hears about everything."

"At least if Plum took Albert, it would be a home," Travis pointed out.

Taylor fought the jittery panic rising in her. "A home?" she questioned, her voice rising shrilly. "A home with Plum the horse killer?"

"What are you talking about?" Travis asked.

Taylor drew Travis over to the side of the hall at the end of a bank of lockers. Lowering her head, she spoke softly so no one would overhear. "When I was over at Westheimer's barn I would hear people talking about Plum, and how the last two horses she'd leased from Ralph had died."

"What do you mean, leased?" Travis asked.

"Plum paid money every month for the upkeep of a horse Ralph owned. She didn't own the horse, but Plum had the right to ride it whenever she wanted. Ralph could use the horse for lessons, but he couldn't let anyone else but Plum take it out on trails or ride it in the corral."

"And the horses she leased died?" Travis checked. "Both of them?"

Taylor nodded.

"How'd she do that?"

"No one knows for sure if it was her fault," Taylor admitted. "One of them had colic and the next one went lame."

"And the people at Ralph's thought it was her fault?" Travis asked.

Taylor nodded. "They said she gave the colic horse grain with mold in it, which caused the colic."

"Why would she do that?" Travis wanted to know.

"I don't think she meant to. I bet she just didn't even look at it before she fed the horse."

"What about the lame horse?" Travis inquired. "How'd she manage that?"

"I heard Ralph's wife complaining to him that Plum rode that horse too hard. She said Plum never cooled either horse down or groomed them afterward. I remember Mrs. Westheimer was really steamed that day because she tried to tell Plum to groom the horse and Plum had mouthed off to her, saying she paid good money for her lease and she shouldn't have to work, too."

"Did someone else groom the horse for her?"

"Ralph or his wife would do it if they saw Plum get off, but a lot of times they were teaching or on a trail ride, and they'd come back to find the horse all sweaty, still saddled, and loosely tied up outside."

"Now I see why you don't want her anywhere near Albert," Travis remarked.

"There's no way I'm going to let that happen. The Westheimers refused to lease another horse to her. I heard she was riding over at Ross River Ranch now."

"But if she wants Albert, how can you stop it?" Travis questioned.

Taylor didn't know how, but it couldn't happen. It just couldn't!

Taylor didn't absorb much learning in school that day. It was nearly impossible to keep her mind on her work while thinking of Albert and Pixie the whole time. Last period was social studies, and as Taylor took her notebook from her locker, she became anxious. She had been so preoccupied with Albert and Pixie over the weekend that she'd slapped her report on Egypt together in less than an hour late Sunday night. She knew it was too short and full of typos.

"See me after class, Taylor," Mr. Romano said the moment she handed the paper to him. One glance had apparently told him it was not well-done.

Taylor smiled weakly. "Okay." On Sunday night she'd convinced herself he'd accept the short, unchecked work, but deep down she'd known he wouldn't.

"Oooooh, *somebody's* in trouble," Jake Richards teased Taylor as she took her assigned seat.

"Yes, and it's going to be you, if you're not quiet," Mr. Romano told Jake.

During class Taylor tried to focus on Mr. Romano's lecture on the conquest of ancient Egypt by the Greek general Alexander the Great. But her mind was really on Albert and Pixie — just as it had been all day long. And as much as she tried to keep from stealing glances at Plum, she found she couldn't resist.

One time Plum sensed Taylor's gaze and turned. Their eyes locked in a cold standoff before Taylor turned away, feeling incredibly awkward.

Taylor began to chew her thumbnail. She'd broken herself of the nail-biting habit in fourth grade by keeping her nails painted with yucky-tasting polish. But in times of deep stress — as in the days just before her parents split up — she reverted to the bad habit. At the moment, though, she wasn't even aware that she was chewing her nail. Taylor's mind was set on something more important. Her mother had made it more than clear that she couldn't keep Albert and Pixie herself. But she had to come up with some plan to keep Plum away from them.

Chapter 9

"Taylor, what's going on with you?" Mr. Romano asked after class. He was standing, leaning on his desk and looking at her with probing eyes.

There was so much Taylor wanted to say. Mr. Romano was a nice guy. She trusted him. But her mouth was dry and no words formed in her mind. Besides, there was no way he could help her with any of her problems.

"Listen, I'm going to be blunt," Mr. Romano said after a few minutes of awkward silence. "Guidance told me your parents split up a few months ago. Is that it?"

Taylor inhaled deeply and considered the question. She had to at least say *something*. "Maybe. I don't know. I miss my dad, but not all the fighting. I wish he'd come around to visit, I guess. It hurts my feelings that he doesn't. And Mom's always stressed about money now. But that's not why I didn't do so well on my report."

Mr. Romano raised a quizzical eyebrow. "Okay, then, what's the reason?"

"Well, you may not think this is a good excuse, but something came up this weekend that I totally didn't expect." She quickly ran through the story about Pixie and Albert. She told him how she'd argued with her mother over keeping them and that it was completely out of the question. "And all I can think about is that they need a home by tomorrow or . . ." Her voice cracked with emotion.

"Or what?" Mr. Romano asked gently.

"The sheriff takes them to auction and anyone could buy them and we wouldn't know what happened to them." Taylor couldn't even bring herself to mention the meat market possibility. Telling Travis about it had turned out to be more painful than she'd expected, and she didn't ever want to talk about it again.

"Could the owners be forced to take them back?" Mr. Romano suggested.

"The sheriff is looking for them, but I don't think anyone knows where they went. Besides, they weren't very good owners to begin with."

Mr. Romano nodded and folded his arms. A faraway look came into his eyes. "I grew up around here, you know. When I was a kid, my sister and I would take trail rides out of a stable down on Wildwood Lane. I forget its name. It's at the bottom of Quail Ridge Road. Do you know it?"

Taylor thought she knew every stable and barn in the area but couldn't think of one at the bottom of Quail Ridge Road. She shook her head. "No. I can't picture it," she replied.

"I remember that they were always taking in strays," Mr. Romano recalled. "Too bad they're not still open."

The fond, distant gaze left his eyes, and Mr. Romano snapped back to the present. "All right, Taylor, I'm going to give you a break." He handed her paper back to her. "You have until Friday to redo this paper with the additional two pages on horses in ancient Egypt."

"Thank you. I'll do a good job this time," Taylor assured him.

"Don't let the horses distract you."

Taylor nodded, though she wasn't sure that was really possible. She was almost to the door when Mr. Romano spoke again. "I just had a thought — Plum Mason rides, doesn't she? Maybe she's looking for a horse."

"Oh . . . I don't think so," Taylor said quickly.

"Are you sure? You might want to ask her," Mr. Romano insisted.

"No. No. I'm sure she isn't looking. Besides, these two are pretty rough-looking. She wouldn't want them."

"I know you two aren't exactly friends. Would you like me to mention it to her?" he offered.

This was terrible! Why had she ever told him?

"No. I don't think she'd be the right kind of owner for this horse," Taylor insisted.

"I see."

With another nod, Taylor left. What did *I see* mean? Did it mean *Yes, I understand. I won't mention it to her*? Or was he implying that she disliked Plum so much that she was going to keep Albert from Plum even if it meant denying him a good home?

And if that last thing was what he'd meant — was it true?

After all, maybe Plum really did just have a run of bad luck with the horses she'd leased.

No. It wasn't possible.

Taylor couldn't believe that Plum could have two horses in a row die like that without being, in some way, responsible.

Taylor arrived home that afternoon just as her mother was rushing out. "You'll never guess who I'm going to see," her mom said excitedly.

"Who?"

"Devon Ross! My catering company was recommended to her, and she might want me to cater a luncheon for her. Can you imagine all the wealthy clients I could pick up from a job like this?"

"That's great! Are you going to her house?"

"No. I'm meeting her at her stable."

"You're going to Ross River Ranch? Cool! Can I come?"

Jennifer considered this a moment but then shook her head. "You'd better not. Bringing my daughter might seem unprofessional."

"Could you ask her if she wants a horse and pony? Free!"

Jennifer cringed slightly, clearly not thrilled with the idea. "I don't even know the woman, Taylor."

"Please!"

"If I can fit it in naturally, I will."

"You won't," Taylor challenged.

"I said if it feels right, I'll do it. Now, don't bug me. I'm nervous enough. This could be big."

"If you get the job, would we have enough money to feed a horse?" Taylor suggested hopefully.

"Taylor!" Jennifer scolded as she planted a kiss on Taylor's head. "Wish me luck," she said, and hurried to her car.

Entering the quiet house, Taylor threw herself onto the couch and lay there. If she could only think hard enough, eventually a solution had to come to her. But what if there was no solution to this?

Taylor hadn't seen her father in a month, but she knew where to find him. He'd still be at his job down at the garage. Maybe he had extra money somewhere — enough to let her board a horse and pony.

Taylor walked outside and went to the side of the

house. She found her bike leaning there. In twenty minutes, she rode into the shopping district of Pheasant Valley, not much more than Maria's Pizzeria, the post office, the Pheasant Valley Pharmacy, Lovely Stems Florist, and Mike's Auto Repair and Gas Station, where her father, Steve Henry, worked for Mike Malone.

"Steve, your kid's here," shouted her father's boss, a bald man with a round belly, when she walked into the front office. "Hey, Taylor, what's new?"

"Know anyone who wants a horse and a pony?" she asked as she walked through the office toward the repair garage.

"Nope," Mike replied. "Who the heck has that kind of dough? Not me, that's for sure."

"Come on, Mike, you're rich," Taylor shot back playfully.

"Yeah, I wish."

Taylor spied her dad working under a car on the farther of two mechanical lifts. His blue jumpsuit was smeared with grease. In the bright fluorescent light, his skin looked extra pale. "Hey, Taylor, what brings you here? You okay?" her dad asked, still working.

The sullen, accusing words *What do you care?* came to mind, but she shoved them aside. "Yeah, I'm okay. I just wanted to say hi, you know?"

He looked down from his work for the first time. "Yeah, well, good to see you. Sorry I haven't been around. I seem to get into a fight with your mom every time I come, so I figured it might be better if I stayed away for a while. Nothing personal to you. You know that, right?"

"Sure."

"How are you and your mom doing?"

"She's working hard. She might have a catering job from Mrs. Ross."

"That rich horsewoman?"

"Yeah, that's her." Taylor figured this was a natural lead-in to the subject of horses. "Guess what Claire and I did last week?"

"Sprang a gorilla being held hostage in someone's basement?" he ventured with a chuckle.

"Not exactly. We rescued a horse and pony, though."

She gave him a quick version of all that had happened, including the threat of Plum Mason. "So, I was wondering if it would be all right with you if I boarded them somewhere. They would be mine . . . ours, I mean. You like to ride, don't you?"

Steve Henry laughed in a way that was not encouraging. "That was a long time ago. It would be fine with me if I had that kind of money — which I don't. What does Mom say?"

"We can't afford it," Taylor mumbled.

"Mom and I have finally hit on something we agree on, then. Sorry, baby; it is most definitely not in the budget."

An unexpected flash of hot anger flared in her. "Then what *is* in your budget?" Taylor asked defiantly. "You don't seem to be paying for anything else."

"Hey!" Steve cried, shaking the greasy wrench he held at her. "Watch that mouth. It's none of your business what I'm paying for. I'm paying plenty. When did you get so fresh?"

"Sorry," Taylor muttered. She had never intended to make him mad. The words had just sparked out.

"I'm sorry, too. When you're older you'll understand. It's tough."

He was right that she didn't understand. Taylor didn't understand why her parents had fought so much that they'd split. She didn't understand why the mere mention of money made both of them blow up all the time. She didn't understand it and she didn't like it — but that was how it was.

"I know how much you love horses," her father went on. "You get that from me. I never had lessons or anything, but back in the day we used to trail ride over at a place . . . oh, what was the name?"

"Was it on Wildwood Lane?" Taylor asked.

"Yeah, how did you know?"

"Mr. Romano told me about it."

"You have John Romano this year? He's a good guy. Yeah, the Romanos went there, too. I think I remember seeing him there once or twice. It was a great place. Too bad it closed."

"Hmm. Too bad," she echoed.

He glanced out the garage window. "It's getting dark earlier these days. I don't want you riding your bike in the dark. Maybe you should get going."

Taylor estimated that she had another two, possibly three hours of reasonably good light left. But she knew he was working and couldn't stand there talking with her much longer.

Steve came to her side and wrapped her in a hug. "I'll come by next week. Okay?"

"Okay," Taylor agreed, not really believing him. She kissed his cheek. "I'll see you then, I guess." Despite her doubts, it was somehow comforting to pretend she thought he was telling the truth.

"Okay. Be good. And sorry I couldn't help you with the horse thing," Steve said as he let her go.

"See you next week," she said with a wave.

Outside, Taylor checked the sky. It wasn't even dusk yet. She had plenty of time to take the long way home. She was sick of going the same old way, seeing the same old scenery.

Pushing off on her bike, she rode out to the stoplight and began to ride up steep Mohegan Lake Road. Before she arrived at the right turn that would take her toward her house, she came to Quail Ridge Road and turned left instead. As soon as she began to ride down the road, she knew she had intended to come this way all along.

Taylor's bike picked up speed as she rode down the hill. Her mother always said, *I never take Quail Ridge if it's icy. Too dangerous.*

Now she saw why.

Taylor was soon going so fast she wasn't sure she could stop. She gripped the handlebars as the road bent one way and then the other. To her right, a low stone wall was all that separated her from a sharp slope leading down to a wooded area.

Pressing on her hand brakes, Taylor attempted to pull back on the bike's ever-increasing speed. All she had to do was get to the bottom where the road turned sharply right and then leveled out. After that, she'd just have to read street signs to find Wildwood Lane.

Taylor was nearly to the bottom of Quail Ridge Road when her front tire slid on gravel. She clutched the handlebars desperately. Her bike went over onto its side, spinning toward the other side of the road.

Chapter 10

Despite the burning pain of her badly skinned knee that throbbed beneath her newly torn jeans, Taylor let out a small snort of laughter when she looked up. She was staring at a bent, rusted street sign overgrown with vines: WILDWOOD LANE. She could barely make out the name beneath all the plant life tangled around the sign. If she hadn't spun all the way across the road and crashed into it, she'd probably never have found the lane.

Taylor winced as she tried to straighten her leg. Reaching out to the signpost for support, she pulled herself up. Although it hurt like crazy when she let go of the post, she *could* stand — which meant her leg wasn't broken, at least.

Grabbing the handlebars of her dented bike, she spun the front wheel with her toe. It turned easily. She was relieved that the bike, although scraped and dinged, was otherwise unharmed. She wheeled it to a tangle of overgrown forsythia bushes that were turning brown and stashed the bike inside its branches.

So this was Wildwood Lane.

She was standing on a narrow dirt road leading off of Quail Ridge. It was just wide enough for one car or truck. Taylor took a step and discovered that her knee buckled slightly, causing her to limp. The pain wasn't unbearable, though, so she continued down the road. No tire tracks marred the dirt, which meant that no one had driven through here at least since the rain last Saturday. Judging from the flatness of the dirt, Taylor guessed no one had been down Wildwood Lane in a very long time. There were only bushes and scrubby trees on either side of the road and for as far as she could see. But the road turned sharply, and she was curious about what lay around the bend.

When Taylor finally turned the corner, she breathed in a slow, awestruck breath. In front of her was the long-abandoned ranch. Blistered wooden buildings and a stable stood silently behind two corrals with broken, splintered fences. Silence hung so thickly over the ranch that Taylor felt she could almost reach out to touch the deep quiet.

Continuing on the dirt road, she came to a large wooden sign that must have once announced the name of the ranch. Now it was so badly faded and peeled that Taylor couldn't read it.

A sudden wind blasted through and shook the loose shutters of the main building. With a bang, a door of another building slammed and made Taylor jump. In the surrounding woods, a loose limb creaked ominously.

Taylor passed a towering maple with knotty roots and widespread branches as she headed to the main building and slid the big front door to one side. She entered a hall with a dirt floor. Even now she inhaled the unmistakable aroma of the horses that had once lived here. To the left was an office, its door hanging off one hinge. A ripped leather couch and a big, badly worn desk were its only furniture.

She guessed that the doorless room to the right, with its many shelves and hooks, was the tack room. When she stepped inside, her sneaker hit something hard. A worn helmet rolled across the room. Picking it up, she lightly brushed it off and sneezed when a cloud of dust was dislodged. Taylor placed the old helmet on a hook and wiped her hands on her jeans.

In the far corner of the tack room floor, someone had left behind a synthetic general-purpose saddle. Taylor squatted to inspect it and saw stirrups still attached. Under the saddle was a filthy saddlecloth.

Leaving the tack room, Taylor moved farther into the shadowy building, walking down the stable's central passage. The only light came from sun that filtered through breaks in the old roof overhead. On either side of her were six box stalls, three on each side, facing one another. Using the corner of her hoodie as a rag, Taylor wiped the grimy bronze nameplates beside each of the six stalls. DAISY. IRISH. MAYA. BUCK. SALU-SUE. And, finally, at the last stall — PRINCE ALBERT.

Was it possible?

Could this have once been Albert's stall? How many horses named Albert could there possibly be?

Taylor did some quick mental math. Rick had said that judging from Albert's teeth he'd estimated Albert was around fifteen years old. Pixie, he'd guessed, was well into her twenties. She knew her dad was thirty-four, and Mr. Romano appeared to be about the same age, more or less.

Albert would have been born when her dad was nineteen. And the colt would have been too young to ride for at least two years, probably three or four years.

Maybe this stall had once belonged to Albert's sire. Though the name might just be a coincidence and not Albert's father at all. Whatever the truth, Taylor was suddenly inspired by the name on the plate. This stall was meant to be Albert's home!

Taking her cell phone from her back pocket, Taylor called Claire but reached only her voice mail. Before she could leave a message, she stopped herself. Mentally, she heard all the adults' reasons why they couldn't leave Pixie and Albert here. They didn't know who owned the place. It would be too much work for Taylor to care for them alone, especially without proper supplies or gear available.

Taylor clicked off the call without saying anything.

Maybe it would be best to simply bring Pixie and Albert here without mentioning it to anyone.

But how would she get them here?

*   *   *

It wasn't easy pedaling up the hill to Claire's house with the old saddle and saddlecloth that she'd strapped onto the basket of her bike with a bungee cord. The dusty old helmet was fastened to the back of the bike with its own chin strap. The added weight of these things threw her horribly off balance, and the climb was difficult enough as it was.

By the time Taylor arrived at Claire's at the top of Mohegan Lake Road, the sky was awash with dusky blues and grays. Claire's van was in the driveway and Claire was beside it. From inside, Bunny barked to greet Taylor. "Bunny and I are taking a walk in the hills. Want to come?" Claire greeted Taylor.

"No, thanks," Taylor declined as she dismounted.

"What's all that?" Claire asked with a nod at the bike.

"A saddle and helmet," Taylor answered. Once again she was unsure how much she should tell Claire. Taylor didn't want Claire to tell her that it wasn't safe or it couldn't be done. As long as Claire didn't say *not* to take Pixie and Albert out for a ride Taylor figured she wouldn't be disobeying. "I found this stuff," she added. "I want to see if I can saddle Albert."

"Don't let Mrs. Kirchner see that you've saddled him," Claire warned, sliding the van door shut and climbing into the driver's side. "She'll have a fit."

"Okay," Taylor agreed.

Claire rolled down the window as she began to pull out of the driveway. "I'd better hurry. There's not much light left. Sure you don't want to come?"

"Sure."

"Okay. The other dogs are all inside, so they won't bother you. Give yourself enough time to ride home before dark."

As soon as Claire left, Taylor wheeled her bike through the gate into the yard. Albert walked out of the run-in shelter and came to her side. Pixie followed. Taylor rubbed his muzzle affectionately, and he responded with a low whicker. She petted Pixie's coarse mane, scratching her crown.

"Everything is going to be okay," Taylor told them softly. "I've found you both a great place to live."

Taylor had mentally mapped out a way to cut through

the woods on horseback — with Pixie following — and ride down to Wildwood Lane. The only time she'd be out in the open would be when she was in the field across from Claire's house, and at the end of the journey, when she needed to cross Quail Ridge Road.

Unstrapping the saddle from her bike basket, Taylor wiped it with one of the white towels until it was reasonably clean. She shook the saddlecloth hard and dust flew everywhere. Pixie sneezed, which made Taylor smile. "Sorry, girl."

"We're going for a ride," Taylor told Albert as she slid the halter over his head. Just before she'd stopped riding at Ralph's, he had shown her how to saddle a horse. She'd done it once by herself while he watched, but she wasn't entirely certain that she could remember how to do it without his guidance.

Taylor placed the saddlecloth slightly forward on Albert's back, toward his withers. Staggering under its weight, Taylor heaved the saddle onto the horse, tugging it back firmly, and then secured the cloth to the saddle.

Dropping the girth, Taylor walked around in *front* of Albert — as Ralph had taught her — to fasten it on the other side. She made sure it wouldn't pinch Albert's skin by sliding the flats of her fingers underneath to check the tightness. Finally, she slid the stirrups down.

Taylor wished she had reins, but for now she had to make do by fastening the lead line to the rings of Albert's halter.

The idea of riding him through the woods made Taylor extremely nervous. But she had to — if she tried to lead them both at a walk, it would be pitch-black by the time she reached Wildwood Lane. As it was, the ride would take about a half hour, maybe more. But she had no intention of going any faster than a walk. She knew there were hiking trails in the woods — the Appalachian Trail that went from Maine to Georgia even cut through in places. Taylor was counting on her memory of where those trails were.

Taylor took the old helmet from the bike. Its satin lining was ripped and flapping. Taylor tore it away completely and discovered a spider sitting in its web. "Enjoy your new home," she said as she tapped it into the grass. Grabbing a towel for a final wipe, Taylor put on the helmet.

After opening the gate, she stuck one foot in the stirrups, swung her other leg up, and mounted. It took only a soft click to get Albert moving. Checking, she didn't see anyone on the street, so she ventured out the gate, confident that Pixie would be behind her.

Once they were down the driveway, they had to walk in the street and past several houses before reaching the field. The *clip-clop* of hooves on the paved road banged like thunder in Taylor's ears. She was sure it was alerting every house she passed that she was riding down the road on horseback. But no one came to a window or door.

Finally, they arrived at the field where they could cut a diagonal line to the woods. "Once we get across this, we'll be hidden from view," Taylor told Albert and Pixie encouragingly.

By shifting her weight and drawing in her makeshift right-hand rein, Taylor steered Albert into the high grass. "Good boy," she praised, pleased that it took so little effort to direct him. As they got closer to the woods, though, Taylor became aware of a figure standing in a shadowy patch.

Riding closer, she realized it was Mrs. Kirchner and her small white dog.

The dog began its shrill yapping, straining on its leash.

"Taylor Henry!" Mrs. Kirchner scolded angrily. "Why

are those creatures still here? Do I have to call the sheriff again? If I have to, I will! You can count on that! And the nerve of you, to run them right through our field. That pony isn't even being ridden. It's running wild. I do not want to be stepping in horse manure in this field."

Taylor was about to say, *Neither of them are running.* But before she could speak, the small dog pulled forward so hard that it yanked the leash from Mrs. Kirchner's hand. In seconds it was yapping aggressively at Albert's ankles.

Albert hopped nervously, neighing. "Whoa, boy," Taylor tried to calm him as she clutched the improvised reins tightly.

Pixie whinnied anxiously.

The dog kept barking as though it had taken up its owner's threatening rant.

Taylor wasn't absolutely certain what happened next, but she had the impression that the dog might have nipped Albert's ankle.

The horse let out an angry cry as he lifted his front legs from the ground and stamped. For a terrible moment, Taylor was sure Albert was going to trample the small dog. Instead, the horse took off at a full gallop.

Chapter 11

The lead line reins flew from Taylor's grip. "Whoa! Whoa!" she shouted, desperately clutching on to the saddle's pommel with one hand and grabbing a handful of black mane with the other. She hung on tight while Albert raced into the woods, crashing past branches, taking small leaps over rocks and logs in his path. Clearly, he didn't like being grabbed by the mane. He swung his head from side to side to get her off.

They came to a narrow creek running through the woods. Albert screeched to a sudden halt, and Taylor flew from his back into the cold, running creek.

Icy water ran down the back of her jacket. It startled

Taylor onto her knees, and as she came up, the chilly water spilled from her helmet, dousing her a second time.

Too panicked to worry about her fall or her soaked clothing, she looked around frantically.

Had Albert and Pixie run off?

Had she lost them?

Taylor was relieved to see Albert grazing on a bush a few yards down the creek. Why had he stopped so suddenly? Had he wanted to eat from that bush, or had the water spooked him? At least he had stayed close. But where was Pixie? "Pixie!" she called, making a gentle clicking sound afterward. "Pixie, here, girl!"

The woods rustled with the gentle sound of breeze-stirred leaves. The creek gurgled along. But Taylor didn't hear any evidence of Pixie moving nearby.

Sloshing her way out of the creek, Taylor called again. This time, the sound of a cracking twig gave her new hope. A minute later, the little pony emerged, breaking through a cluster of boxwood bushes. Her mane and tail strewn with snagged twigs and leaves, Pixie whinnied to Albert as she trotted to his side.

Soaked and aching, Taylor was nonetheless deeply relieved that she hadn't lost Pixie and Albert. The idea of having to explain to Claire — and to the sheriff! — that she'd lost a horse and pony in the woods was just too awful to think about.

She saw a metal marker nailed on a tree and smiled. Taylor had accidentally stumbled on the part of the well-traveled Appalachian Trail that she'd hoped to find.

After a careful remount, a click, and a knee squeeze, they were moving once again. Taylor was pretty sure she could guide them through the woods that ran behind Mohegan Lake Road all the way down to Quail Ridge Road. As they moved along, she felt confident they were going in the right direction.

A cold shiver ran down Taylor's spine, and she zipped her hoodie all the way up. It didn't help much because she was still soaked. At least Pixie and Albert would have a proper shelter for the night if the temperature plummeted as, she now remembered, the weather report had predicted it would.

Peering through the trees, Taylor spied a path to her right that descended gradually toward Quail Ridge Road, and she turned Albert toward it. "Come on, Pixie," she called with a broad wave of her arm.

Pixie's ears swiveled toward Taylor and she moved once more. It wasn't much longer before they reached the edge of the trees and came out onto Quail Ridge. After checking for cars, Taylor quickly crossed them to Wildwood Lane. "Almost home," she encouraged the horses as they went down the dirt road to the ranch.

As she rode Albert past the faded sign, Taylor imagined she was a cowgirl riding into some deserted ghost town in the Wild West. She halted in front of the main building and lowered herself from Albert's back. There were three-sided covered stalls that faced the outdoors against the right wall of this main building, but since Pixie and Albert were the only ones there, she decided to give them the bigger, warmer stalls inside.

Pushing the sliding front door once more, she tried something new. With her fingers to her lips, she whistled, curious to see if they would come. Taylor smiled with delight as they instantly walked toward her. "Good going, you guys," she praised them. She made a mental note to bring treats when she came back.

Inside, the stalls were very dark now. The slats of light that had illuminated the place before had all died away. Only the last gray rays of daylight coming through the wide-open front doorway made it possible to see at all.

Taylor was suddenly aware that there was no hay, but the animals had been fed at Claire's, so they were probably okay for now. They'd drunk a lot of water at the creek, which was good, since she doubted this place had running water.

Taylor placed her hand on Albert's chest to check his temperature. It seemed normal. Pixie wasn't sweaty, either. To double-check, she looked closely at Albert's nostrils to see if they were flaring from exertion, but they weren't. Neither were Pixie's. They'd probably be okay until she could get some brushes and other grooming tools. All they'd done was walk, after all — if she didn't count Albert's short sprint.

Taylor knew their hooves should be picked clean. She lifted Albert's back hoof and saw it was caked with mud and pebbles. With her finger she dislodged some of it, but she needed a hoof pick to do the job properly.

Oh, this is crazy, Taylor thought. *What was I thinking?* Where was she going to get grooming brushes, a hoof pick, hay, and oats? Never mind a bridle or a saddle! She didn't have a job. Both her parents had already told her plainly that they couldn't afford a horse.

As she was worrying about all this, someone stepped out of the office area and shone a blinding flashlight right into Taylor's eyes.

Chapter 12

"Who is there?" a woman's voice demanded forcefully.

The light moved closer. Taylor shielded her eyes with her hand, heart pounding. What kind of trouble was she in? Could this be a private security guard or a sheriff's deputy?

Albert whinnied anxiously as the light hit his eyes.

"Have you brought a horse in here?" the voice demanded.

The approaching figure was now close enough for Taylor to see. She was immediately relieved that the woman wore no uniform of any kind. She was petite and wore glasses. The glare of the flashlight bounced off the lenses, hiding her eyes. But judging from the rest of the face, Taylor estimated that she was somewhere in her sixties.

"Is this your ranch?" Taylor asked.

"It is," the woman replied. "I am Mrs. LeFleur, the owner. And who, may I ask, are you?"

Before Taylor could answer, Mrs. LeFleur screamed and jumped away, dropping her light on the ground.

Taylor bent to retrieve it. In the flashlight's beam she saw that Pixie was right behind the woman.

Mrs. LeFleur placed her hand to her head as if to assure herself that she was still in one piece. "You have two creatures, I take it," she remarked breathlessly.

"She's a pony. Pixie won't hurt you," Taylor assured her.

"A horse *and* a pony, I see. Well, why are they here?"

"They need a place to stay." Taylor then gave Mrs. LeFleur a quick version of how she'd come into possession of Pixie and Albert. "And I thought this place was empty and I could keep them here. I didn't know you owned it," she concluded.

"If you had come here yesterday, I wouldn't have owned it," Mrs. LeFleur said.

"You mean you just bought it today?" Taylor asked.

"Inherited it," Mrs. LeFleur corrected her. "I inherited it from an uncle, but I had to fight for it in court. Apparently it was about to become an unclaimed property because no one could locate me to claim the inheritance. It was going to be sold to pay off back taxes, and someone named Mrs. Ross was all set to buy it."

"I know who Mrs. Ross is. My mother is at her place right now," Taylor revealed.

"Well, she's no friend of mine. I don't like someone trying to scoop my inheritance right out from under me."

"No, I guess not," Taylor sympathized. She still held the flashlight, and she saw that the woman was looking her over.

"You're quite young, aren't you?" Mrs. LeFleur observed.

"Thirteen."

"Are you usually such a mess?"

Taylor had to laugh at the truthfulness of the blunt question. Her jeans were ripped and her skinned knee was evident. She was soaked. Only a small amount of hair remained in her ponytail; the rest stuck out from under the horrible old helmet in clumps. "I guess I could use a shower," she admitted.

"Indeed so," the woman agreed. "Clearly you've had a time of it."

Taylor's cell phone buzzed, telling her she had a text message from Claire.

PIX & AL R GONE! W/U? CALL ME ASAP!

"I should have told Claire what I planned to do, I guess," Taylor realized. "Mrs. LeFleur, how much would it cost to board Pixie and Albert here?" Taylor asked.

"Here?" Mrs. LeFleur asked with a note of disbelief. "You must be kidding! It's in no condition to house horses. Look at it!"

"It's better than a front yard with only an old pool cover over their heads. That's where they're living now. Before that they were living in a dark building where no one even let them out. This would be the best place they've been in a long while," Taylor said.

Mrs. LeFleur sighed as she glanced indecisively from Albert to Pixie. "Poor creatures," she said softly before turning back to Taylor. "I haven't even decided if I'm going to reopen the place. There's such an awful lot of work to be done."

"It's a great ranch, though. I can picture it all fixed

up. My dad and my teacher both told me it used to be the best place."

"Mmm," said Mrs. LeFleur. "I remember it, too. It *was* wonderful."

"Could I leave Pixie and Albert here at least for tonight?" Taylor asked. "It's too dark to bring them back now, and I don't have a trailer."

"All right. Tell your friend where you are and that you have the horses," Mrs. LeFleur suggested. "You should put them next to each other in adjacent stalls so they won't feel lonely." She shone her flashlight around.

"It's funny you picked that stall," Taylor commented. "Look at the nameplate."

"'Prince Albert,'" Mrs. LeFleur read. "What an amazing coincidence. I think you should change Albert's name to Prince Albert. He seems like a princely fellow to me."

"I think I will," Taylor agreed.

"Wait a minute," Mrs. LeFleur said. She walked inside the stall and took off one of her chunky-heeled shoes. Using the thick heel as a hammer, she forcefully whacked a sharp nail that protruded from the wall. Then she checked for others.

"All right. It's safe to bring your pony in here after you unsaddle the big guy. There's no proper bedding for them in either stall, but they're clean enough except for a few spiderwebs."

Taylor ran the stirrups back up the saddle to the stirrup bar. She undid the girth and placed it over the saddle. Holding the saddle and the saddlecloth together, she moved them backward, lifting them off Albert. "Where should I put this?" she asked Mrs. LeFleur.

"We can put it in the tack room after you get these two to bed."

Taylor steered Albert — now Prince Albert — into the stall by pushing him gently with her hand. As expected, Pixie tried to follow him in. It took some firm pushing to redirect her to the stall next door. "I'll be back in the morning," she assured them. "Be good."

"If you don't mind," Mrs. Le Fleur requested as Taylor came out of the stall and latched the gate behind her, "I'd like to talk to you a little bit before you leave."

"I don't mind," Taylor said as she began sending a text message back to Claire. "What do you want to talk to me about?"

"I've been sitting in that dark office wondering whether I should sell this place or not. I was hoping for some kind of sign that would tell me what I should do — and then you and your animals showed up."

"You think *I'm* your sign?" Taylor inquired.

Mrs. LeFleur nodded. "Maybe. Plus, you're very persuasive. You've got me thinking that this place could have possibilities."

Mrs. LeFleur stood the flashlight on end so that it pointed to the ceiling and illuminated the entire office in a dim light. She sat lightly on the edge of the desk. Taylor faced her, seated on the old, torn couch.

"I haven't ridden in thirty years," Mrs. LeFleur said. "But I used to love it."

"I bet it would all come back to you," Taylor said. "It's probably like riding a bicycle. Once you know how, you never forget."

"I don't really have the large amount of money required to repair this place," Mrs. LeFleur said. "It makes more sense just to sell it, but somehow I feel that I want to keep it."

"Oh, you have to keep it," Taylor insisted.

Mrs. LeFleur smiled, just a little. "Is that so? Why do I *have* to keep it?"

Because Pixie and Albert need a place to live, and this place would be perfect if you could fix it up. That was the thought that sprang to Taylor's mind, but she decided it might be best to keep it to herself. She needed something more persuasive. "It's a great place. You love to ride. And it just sort of came to you like it was meant to be yours."

"That's all true," Mrs. LeFleur agreed. "But I'm not rich like that Mrs. Ross. I can't keep a ranch going just for my own entertainment. It would have to make money."

"You could board horses and offer classes," Taylor suggested quickly.

"I couldn't afford to pay anyone."

"I would help you — for free — just for the chance to be near the horses. You could offer pony rides on Pixie. Albert's really easy to ride and gentle. He'd be a great lessons horse. I'm not a great rider, but I know enough to teach little kids."

"It's really fascinating that there was a Prince Albert nameplate here already," Mrs. LeFleur said. "So now he's become a prince. Perhaps he was a prince all along. It's another sign, I'd say."

"A sign of what?" Taylor asked.

"That he belongs here, of course."

"Yes!" Taylor said, encouraged. "Yes, it does seem that way." She didn't know if it was a sign or not — she wasn't even sure if she believed that signs of this kind had any meaning at all — but she could tell that Mrs. LeFleur did. And because of these *signs*, she was leaning toward keeping the place and allowing Pixie and Albert to stay.

"You know, I did meet a lovely young lady in the deli yesterday, and we got to talking. I asked her for directions to Wildwood Lane, and she told me all about how her grandmother had once been a horse instructor at the ranch when it was open. She asked if I was reopening it and said she would like to give lessons if I was."

"What's her name?" Taylor asked.

"I can't recall but she wrote down her name and number." Mrs. LeFleur took a folded paper napkin from her pocket and read from it. "Daphne Chang. Do you know her?"

"I know who she is. She goes to the high school."

"I could get in touch with her, I suppose," Mrs. LeFleur considered.

Car headlights glared through the front window and lit up the office for a moment before snapping off. In the next moment, Taylor's mother and Claire walked into the office. Jennifer held a flashlight. "I forgot all about this place," she said, gazing around. "I haven't been here since I was a kid."

Claire put a blue five-gallon jug of bottled water on the desk. "I brought this for Albert and Pixie," she explained. "I have a bale of hay in the van."

Taylor got off the couch and stood. "Mom, Claire, this is Mrs. LeFleur. She's going to open this place up again."

Taylor looked eagerly to Mrs. LeFleur for confirmation of this. Mrs. LeFleur's gently wrinkled face took on a new youthfulness as she broke into a radiant smile. "Yes, I am. Indeed, I am. Somehow I'm going to make this work," she said. "Don't ask me how, of course. I'll have to worry about that later. But I think this is clearly meant to be, and when things are meant to be they just somehow fall into place. Don't you think so?"

"Sometimes," Jennifer allowed tentatively. Taylor could tell her mother wasn't convinced that things always worked out for the best.

"I'm with you!" Claire told Mrs. LeFleur with much more enthusiasm than Jennifer had shown. "I remember how great this ranch used to be. It could be that way again!"

Taylor looked at Claire and smiled. She felt she could read her mind. Taylor was sure that Claire already had plans to populate the ranch with all her strays and rescues, starting with Albert and Pixie.

"Who actually owns those animals?" Mrs. LeFleur asked Claire.

"The sheriff put me in contact with the owner just a few hours ago," Claire revealed. "She doesn't want them, and she's agreed to mail me their ownership papers."

"The owner is just giving them to you?" Mrs. LeFleur questioned.

"She's lucky she escaped a criminal neglect charge," Claire said. "I should have the papers by the end of the week."

"How much would it cost to buy Albert and Pixie from you once you have the papers?" Mrs. LeFleur asked.

"Ask Taylor. I'm giving the papers to her," Claire replied.

Taylor's jaw dropped. She was going to become Pixie and Albert's owner!

Jennifer shook her head. "Wait a minute, Claire, I've already told Taylor that we don't have the money to —"

Claire interrupted by putting her hand on Jennifer's arm. "Maybe Taylor and Mrs. LeFleur could come to some arrangement," she suggested. "What if Taylor could ride Albert whenever she wanted, but she'd have to work at the ranch for his upkeep? Mrs. LeFleur could use Albert for trail rides and lessons. That way Albert would be paying for his own upkeep, too."

"Taylor has already suggested something similar," Mrs. LeFleur said, "and I think it's a wonderful idea."

"What about Pixie?" Taylor asked Mrs. LeFleur.

Mrs. LeFleur sighed uncertainly but did not answer.

Taylor barely dared to breathe as she waited for Mrs. LeFleur's response. What would she do if the woman didn't want Pixie? Was it better for one of them to have a home rather than have both of them be homeless? But it would be too heartbreaking to split them apart. She looked to Claire for help, but Claire's face was blank and impossible to read.

"I'm sure she's a sweet pony. But will I make enough

on pony rides to justify the upkeep?" Mrs. LeFleur wondered.

"Small children like to take beginning lessons on ponies," Taylor offered.

Mrs. LeFleur nodded thoughtfully. "Well, we can give it a try, can't we?"

"I'm sure all the kids will like her," Taylor said excitedly.

"Do you know any other young people who would be willing to work in exchange for free riding time?" Mrs. LeFleur asked.

"Not really," Taylor admitted. "But I'll find some. I'll ask in school."

"Do that, and I'll phone Daphne Chang. I'll also inquire at the local high schools," Mrs. LeFleur said. She turned to Jennifer. "Can I assume Taylor has your permission for all this?"

"As long as it doesn't interfere with schoolwork," she said.

Taylor went to her mother and hugged her. "Thank you! Thank you! It won't get in the way. I promise!"

"It had better not," Jennifer warned seriously.

"No, it really won't."

"Tomorrow morning I'll bring down the food and other things I have for Pixie and Albert," Claire said.

Taylor longed to be there in the morning to start getting the place into shape. It was on the tip of her tongue to ask to skip school the next day, but she thought better of it. She had just promised not to let this get in the way of her grades.

"I'll come over straight after school," she promised Mrs. LeFleur. "I'm just going to go say good night to Pixie and Albert . . . I mean Prince Albert."

Taylor flew out the door and ran down the wide space leading to the stalls, giddy with happiness. "We did it! We did it!" Taylor told Pixie and Albert in a thrilled whisper.

They looked at her from above the gates of their new stalls. Lines of silver moonlight now beamed through the slats in the broken roof, lighting the two of them in a shimmering, magic-seeming glow.

Taylor rested her forehead on Albert's muzzle and rubbed his cheek. "Don't you worry. I'm going to make sure this works. This is going to be the happiest home you've had yet. I promise. After all, you're a prince now."

Chapter 13

"Travis, you have to come to the ranch with me today, okay?" Taylor said on Tuesday morning as she taped one of her flyers to her locker. The night before, she had stayed up late designing and printing them from the family computer.

"Why? So I can work for free?" asked Travis. He ripped off another piece of tape and handed it to her. "No, thank you. Besides, there's a classic X-Men comic auction on eBay today. I don't want to miss it. My mom's letting me use her PayPal account. Do you realize how big that is? She's never done that before."

"Ah, come on, Travis. There's always some auction happening on eBay. Come with me."

"Albert and Pixie don't even like me," Travis argued.

"They'll like you once they get to know you better," Taylor said.

She stepped back to admire her flyer.

NEW PHEASANT VALLEY RANCH OPENING!!!!!
CHANCE OF A LIFETIME TO
HORSEBACK RIDE FOR FREE!
JOIN THE NEW WORKING STUDENT PROGRAM!
SPEND TIME AROUND HORSES AND
LEARN ALL ABOUT THEM!
SEE TAYLOR HENRY FOR DETAILS
CELL PHONE 555-987-4901

"What's the Working Student Program?" Travis asked. "Did you just make that up?"

Taylor smiled, feeling just a little embarrassed. "Sort of," she admitted. "But it makes sense. If you work around horses, you'll learn stuff about them."

"It sounds like they'll get riding lessons in exchange for the work," Travis argued.

"No, it doesn't."

"Yes, it does," Travis insisted.

128

"Well, it says right here to get in touch with me. When they call or text or whatever, I'll tell them that they're not getting free lessons," Taylor said, slightly peeved at Travis for being so argumentative, and also knowing he was probably right. "No one will mind. People like me who love horses are happy just to be *around* horses."

"Okay. Don't get mad," he said.

"I'm not mad," Taylor told him, calming down. "So will you help us at the ranch or not?"

"I really don't want to miss that auction, plus I have a lot of homework."

The buzzer for their first class sounded. "I have homework, too," Taylor said, reminding herself to try to get as much of it done during skills class as possible. "You don't have to stay there all night."

"I'll let you know at lunch," he answered, turning a hallway corner. With a wave, he disappeared down the crowded hall.

Feeling optimistic, Taylor was aware of a bounce in her step that hadn't been there for a while. Things were really looking up. Her mother had gotten the catering job at Ross River Ranch. Taylor would soon take ownership of her own horse and pony, and she was about to embark on the adventure of being involved with a new horse ranch. Life was looking extremely good to her.

Taylor was nearly to class when Plum came up behind her. "Do you have that phone number for me?" she asked.

"Oh, um . . . I think Claire had her phone shut off," Taylor lied. "There's no way to get in touch with her."

"Are you kidding?" Plum cried. "Didn't she pay her bill?"

Taylor shrugged. "Who knows?" She walked to class, leaving Plum in the hall looking annoyed. Despite her high spirits, Taylor felt a twinge of anxiety. She would feel a lot safer when Prince Albert's and Pixie's ownership papers arrived.

That afternoon Taylor pedaled her bike down Wildwood Lane, fretting about how to tell Mrs. LeFleur that she hadn't been able to recruit a single helper. The few girls who had inquired about her flyers became instantly uninterested when they learned that there was only one horse and one pony there and that no lessons were being offered. But when Taylor turned the bend, her spirits lifted. The ghost town feeling of the day before had been replaced with a whirl of activity.

Pixie and Prince Albert were in the first corral grazing on clumps of grass around the fence. A slim girl of about sixteen or so was looking them over. Long, silky black hair cascaded down her back. Taylor knew right away that she was Daphne Chang. The girl had been student body president at PV Middle School. She and Taylor had never met, but Taylor had always admired her style and confidence.

A van with writing on its side and a pickup truck were parked by the main building. Five men were at work on the outside of the building, scraping blistered, peeling paint and sandpapering the sliding door. Out behind the main building, Taylor heard the repetitive banging of a hammer.

Taylor leaned her bike against the huge maple tree between the corral and the main building. She lifted the plastic bag of apples she'd brought out of the front basket and then climbed up onto the corral railing. "Hi," she greeted Daphne.

Prince Albert immediately caught the aroma of apples

and walked over to Taylor, bumping her bag with his muzzle. She laughed and dug one from the bag, presenting it to him with a flattened palm.

"Don't you go to PV Middle School?" Daphne said, approaching Taylor.

"Yes," Taylor said, feeling good that Daphne was even aware of her. "I'm in the eighth grade. I'm Taylor Henry."

"I'm Daphne Chang," the girl said with a smile. "I'm going to give lessons here once Mrs. Le Fleur officially opens."

"Awesome!" Taylor said. "Would you use Pixie and Albert?"

Daphne nodded. "Mrs. LeFleur said it would be okay with you. Is that true?"

"Absolutely. It's part of my deal for keeping them here. Do you have a horse?"

"Yeah, I have her boarded over at Ross River Ranch. But my parents make me pay for it, and it's getting way too expensive. I don't know how much longer I can afford it. Maybe when this place is ready I'll bring her over here. Her name is Mandy. She's a gray mare, mostly barb with a little quarter horse blood in her, too."

"I don't know that breed, barb," Taylor admitted.

"A barb is an ancient North African desert breed, like an Arabian but more sturdy, less high-strung."

"What style do you ride?" Taylor asked.

"English. I did competitive jumping on Mandy last year."

"No way!" Taylor gasped, impressed beyond words. "Would you give lessons in jumping?"

"Sure, if the student was ready for it. You have to be a really solid rider before you start jumping, though. Do you jump?"

"Oh, no, not at all. I ride Western style. But I would *love* to learn English. I really want to jump someday."

"Maybe I can get you started."

"I'd have to save up some money to pay you first."

Daphne waved her concerns away. "I wouldn't expect to get paid, not if we're all working here at the barn together."

"That would be so great," Taylor said. She swung her legs over the fence and jumped down the other side.

"I brought a saddle and bridle but it's English. Want to try it?" Daphne offered.

Before Taylor could say that she would love to, a strange girl about her own age stormed out of the front building and strode purposefully toward them. In her hand was a coiled red-and-white-striped lead line.

The scowling girl was slim, but unlike graceful Daphne, she was all sharp angles. She had very dark brown hair that fell to her shoulders beneath a red baseball cap, a plaid flannel shirt, and jeans tucked into work boots. "*There* are my animals!" she cried. "Who said you could take them outside?"

Taylor and Daphne answered the girl at the same time.

"*Your* animals?" Taylor cried.

"Who said I couldn't?" Daphne asked.

"I was just assembling my tools to give them a good grooming, and when I returned for them they weren't in their stalls," the girl complained. "Now I need them back."

"Wait a minute. Who are you, anyway?" Daphne asked.

"And these animals are mine, not yours, by the way," Taylor quickly added. "I'm picking up their papers this evening."

134

The girl threw back her shoulders, puffed up with her own self-importance. "I'm Mercedes Gonzalez, and Mrs. LeFleur has appointed me Junior Barn Manager. I live just up the road, so I can be here whenever I'm needed."

"When did Mrs. LeFleur do that?" Taylor asked. Mercedes's overbearing, bossy approach had definitely rubbed Taylor the wrong way. "And why did you call them *your* animals? They're not yours."

"Mrs. LeFleur recruited me from the guidance office at Pheasant Valley High today. I'm a freshman there. My guidance counselor knows that I ride and called me down to meet Mrs. LeFleur," Mercedes replied.

Taylor wondered why she'd never seen this girl at school. She would have been just one year ahead of Taylor when she was back in the middle school.

"Albert is *my* horse and Pixie is *my* pony," Taylor repeated.

"That's not what Mrs. LeFleur told *me*," Mercedes disagreed. "She said that they're owned under a sort of joint agreement between their owner and the barn. I called them *my* animals because they're under my management. And since I have been given the job of running this place, I say that these animals may not be ridden until they are properly groomed. The plumber has just finished reattaching the water lines to the well and we have running water, so I would like to clean them."

Taylor and Daphne looked at each other. "What a tyrant," Daphne murmured.

"I know," Taylor agreed. "But she's probably right about grooming them."

"Probably," Daphne agreed quietly. She turned back to Mercedes and spoke to her in a louder voice. "All right. Where would you like me to bring them, boss?"

The way Daphne called Mercedes *boss* made Taylor smile.

Mercedes pointed to one of the smaller buildings to the right of the main one. "There's a wash stall in there with two big sinks and a hose," she said. Then she opened the gate and approached Prince Albert, holding the clip to the lead line toward his bridle.

Prince Albert neighed a warning to her and Mercedes stepped back, alarmed.

Taylor glanced at the red baseball cap on Mercedes's head. It occurred to her that the nice thing to do would be to tell Mercedes to take it off.

Taylor just couldn't bring herself to do the nice thing.

Mercedes approached Prince Albert again, and this time the horse stomped his foot at her, intimidating her into taking several more steps back.

Taylor went to Mercedes's side and reached her hand out. "Let me try," she offered.

Mercedes tilted her head and studied Taylor suspiciously. "Horses usually like me," she said, still holding on to the lead line.

Taylor shrugged and kept her hand extended.

"I didn't even have to put a line on either of them," Daphne put in. "I just let them follow me out of their stalls."

"That wasn't very safe," Mercedes said huffily.

Daphne rolled her dark eyes. "Whatever. I got them into the corral without a problem, didn't I?"

Prince Albert sputtered at Mercedes. Pixie came to his side and turned her back toward the girl.

"Fine," Mercedes relented, placing the lead line clip into Taylor's hand and passing her the coil.

"Maybe you had better step back," Taylor warned Mercedes.

Mercedes glared at Taylor, but she stepped farther away as Taylor approached Prince Albert and clipped the line to his halter without any problem. "Good boy," she praised him, stroking his muzzle. With her free hand she soothed Pixie by rubbing her neck.

"I'll meet you at the wash stall," Mercedes said, walking toward the corral gate.

"Wow! Pixie and Prince Albert really don't like her," Daphne remarked once Mercedes was too far away to hear. "That makes four of us."

Taylor chuckled lightly. She felt glad Daphne was there. Taylor wouldn't have wanted to come up against the formidable Mercedes on her own.

A pang of guilt hit Taylor about not telling Mercedes what she knew about Prince Albert's and Pixie's reaction to the baseball cap. It was on the tip of her tongue to tell Daphne, but she decided not to tell her, either. She seemed great but they had just met. Taylor couldn't be sure Daphne would keep her secret.

And this was a secret Taylor wanted kept. Mercedes was *way* too into taking charge for Taylor's liking. Taylor had found this place. It was *she* who had brought Mrs. LeFleur her *sign* and convinced her to open the ranch again. Prince Albert and Pixie were *hers*. The fact that they had come into her possession and she had found a way to keep them was practically a miracle. Taylor was not going to let some bossy know-it-all like Mercedes take it out of her hands.

Taylor decided she would have to talk to Mrs. LeFleur about the ownership arrangement. She supposed that in a way they *were* co-owners, since Mrs. LeFleur was going to house and feed them. Taylor would feel better when they'd ironed out the exact arrangements.

In the meantime, Mercedes needed to be seriously calmed down. Prince Albert's and Pixie's fear of people in baseball caps was just the hedge Taylor needed to stay in control and not have Mercedes take charge of them.

Chapter 14

Taylor led Prince Albert up to the bath stall, with Pixie following behind. When they were near, Mercedes came around from the back of the building and pulled open the two double doors so Taylor could enter with the horses.

Taylor brought them inside, stepping onto a rough cement floor. To her left was a stall with no front gate and two metal rings bolted onto either side. Each ring had a nylon line clipped to it with another clip on the end that dangled to the floor. She had never seen a setup like this. At Ralph's she had groomed her horse outside.

Mercedes came to the door but hung back, clearly nervous about getting too close to Albert and Pixie. "Well, what are you waiting for?" she barked harshly. "Tie Prince Albert into the stall."

Taylor led him in and looped his lead line into the ring to her right.

"Unclip the lead line and tie him with the ropes attached to the rings. That's what they're there for," Mercedes corrected her.

Taylor attached the lines to the rings on either side of Albert's halter. "Now what?" she asked Mercedes.

"Haven't you ever bathed a horse before?"

"No," Taylor admitted. She had groomed horses after riding them at Ralph's barn, but she'd never *bathed* one. She picked up a hose from the floor and began to spray Prince Albert. He neighed unhappily.

"You don't just spray them full blast with a hose," Mercedes said in the same superior tone that seemed to be her trademark. "Stick your finger in it so it's more of a gentle spray. And don't do it until you're ready. You don't want your horse standing there catching a chill while you're getting your stuff together. First, put some Mane and Tail into a bucket."

"Mane and Tail?" Taylor asked, annoyed but also relieved that Mercedes was there to help.

"It's the brand of horse shampoo I brought. It's over there by the bucket. Put some shampoo in and fill the bucket in that sink."

"Is there a sponge?"

"Didn't you bring your own grooming kit?" Mercedes asked.

"I don't have one," Taylor replied.

"What?" Mercedes cried. "What have you been using?"

"The truth is, I just got Prince Albert and Pixie," Taylor told her. She quickly revealed everything that had happened over the past four days.

Mercedes surprised Taylor by laughing so hard she had to lean against the door, clutching her sides. "Four days! And you had them in someone's front yard?" she said breathlessly. "That is too funny!"

Mercedes's hilarious laughter was contagious, making Taylor smile despite her dislike of the girl. "It wasn't *that* funny," she said.

"No! No!" Mercedes said, calming down. "The funny part is that I thought you'd owned them for *years* and that you were the one who had let them get into this state. I'd decided I despised whoever owned them — and all the while you and your friend were the ones who rescued them. So it turns out I don't hate *you* at all!"

"Gee, thanks a lot," Taylor said wryly.

"No, really. It was just a misunderstanding," Mercedes insisted. "Guess we got off to a bad start. Sorry I got you all wrong."

Taylor opened her mouth to speak, but no words came out. She wasn't quite sure what to say — so she said the only thing that came to mind.

"Pixie and Prince Albert don't really dislike you; they're just afraid of your baseball cap."

Daphne came out of the main building and let out a low, admiring whistle when she saw Prince Albert and Pixie. "I guess you were right, Mercedes," she admitted. "They were dirtier than I thought. They look so much better."

Mercedes beamed with pride. "They still need new shoes," she said. "Prince Albert, especially, has overgrown his. Does anyone know a good farrier?"

"Mrs. Ross has an awesome farrier who comes every

week to check her horses," Daphne told them. "I'll get his number the next time I'm there."

"That Ross River Ranch looks gorgeous from the road," Taylor mentioned.

"It is," Daphne confirmed.

"I had a gorgeous stable once," Mercedes said wistfully, "and five horses."

"You did?" Taylor asked, impressed.

"Uh-huh, but it's all gone now."

"What happened?" Daphne inquired.

"Stupid adult stuff," Mercedes said, waving her hand as if to shoo away bad memories. "It doesn't matter."

"So, did you just recently move to Pheasant Valley?" Taylor asked.

"Yeah. What a dump, huh?" Mercedes replied.

Taylor and Daphne once again exchanged wry glances. "We kind of like it, actually," Daphne said.

Mercedes shrugged. "Whatever. I guess I'll get used to it. It's just that it's not Weston, where I used to live, and I miss my horses."

Mrs. LeFleur joined them, clapping her hands in delight when she saw Pixie's and Prince Albert's shining coats. "My, my! Look at them. Aren't they beautiful! Beautiful! Who would have thought it?"

Mrs. LeFleur was exaggerating just a bit. Prince Albert's ribs still protruded, and Pixie wore the same frazzled, unkempt mane — but it was much cleaner. Mercedes had helped Taylor braid Prince Albert's mane, but Pixie wouldn't stand still for it. Both of their coats gleamed. The grooming session had improved their appearance a lot; there was no denying it.

Mrs. LeFleur sighed. "Oh, there's just so much to do. It seems overwhelming."

"We'll all work and it'll get done," Taylor assured her. "I just wish there were more of us." She glanced toward the entrance of the ranch to see if Travis was coming, but he wasn't there.

Chapter 15

A week later, Taylor had Prince Albert tied in place in the central passage of the main building with halter ropes on either side so she could groom him one last time before Daphne arrived to teach a private lesson, her very first one.

In the week just past, Wildwood Stables — so far no one had come up with any other name for the ranch that everyone could agree upon — had been a hive buzzing with activity. The roof had been covered with new plywood and shingles. A fresh coat of red paint had been applied. Mrs. LeFleur had hired an electrician to rewire the place and bring it up to the state safety code. After that, she announced, she was flat out of money, at least until they could get in some horse boarders.

Daphne, Mercedes, and Taylor had worked together feverishly to fix up the box stalls, finally laying in a bedding of wood shavings in Prince Albert and Pixie's adjacent stalls.

"I know you'll do great," Taylor told Prince Albert. "We want everyone to see what a terrific school horse you are. You'll be in demand, and everyone will want to take lessons on you. That way Mrs. LeFleur will see that you're invaluable and won't mind that you eat like . . . like a horse." In truth, Albert ate more than most horses. Even in one week his once-protruding ribs were now much less visible. Taylor wondered if this was because he'd once been nearly starved. She was hoping his voracious appetite would slow down once he attained his former weight.

During the week, she'd had a serious talk with Mrs. LeFleur about the details of sharing ownership of Prince Albert and Pixie. Mrs. LeFleur was happy to pick up all the expenses in return for Taylor's weekly work. But she made one exception clear — if Prince Albert and Pixie could not be used for lessons because they weren't good with the students, then Mrs. LeFleur would be forced to return full ownership to Taylor and charge for their board. "I just can't afford their upkeep if I can't use them for lessons and rides," Mrs. LeFleur had said apologetically. "It's not because I want to be mean."

"I know you're not mean, Mrs. LeFleur," Taylor had replied. "You've been great. *Really.*"

Mrs. LeFleur had nodded. "Let's hope for the best. I'm sure it will be fine."

So today would be Prince Albert's first test. He had to be gentle and patient, sensible, and cooperative. Taylor knew he was all those things, so there was *no* need to worry.

Taylor tacked up using an almost-new general-purpose saddle and a comfortable snaffle-bit bridle that Daphne didn't use anymore and had generously donated. Mrs. LeFleur had bought the thick blue saddle blanket.

Unhooking Prince Albert, Taylor led him out of the main building and toward the nearest corral where Daphne waited with a blonde girl of about eight who was dressed for riding with a helmet, a fitted jacket, leggings, and proper heeled shoes.

"Meet Prince Albert," Taylor said.

"Pet him, Maddy." Daphne urged her new student gently forward. But as the girl reached out, Prince Albert neighed and turned his back toward her.

"That's not a very princely way to act," Taylor scolded him mildly. She spoke to Maddy. "He's really very nice once you get to know him."

Maddy walked around toward Prince Albert's front to try again. This time Prince Albert snorted at the girl and stomped his foot.

"Albert!" Taylor scolded him. "What's wrong with you?"

"Is he afraid of riding helmets as well as baseball caps?" Daphne asked.

"No, I've worn a helmet all this week while I've ridden him."

"Let's see if he'll let me ride him," Daphne suggested. She approached and, holding the saddle, she put her foot in the stirrup. Prince Albert neighed and stepped away, forcing Daphne to jump back.

"That's not nice," Taylor scolded him.

Taylor turned to Daphne. "Maybe some part of his tack is bothering him." Taylor checked over Prince Albert's saddle, harness, and bridle. She opened his mouth to make sure nothing was broken on the two D-rings of the jointed bit. "It seems fine," she reported.

"Try petting him again," Daphne suggested to Maddy.

Again, Prince Albert turned away from the girl.

"See if he'll let you ride him, Taylor," Daphne said.

Nodding, Taylor stuck her foot in the stirrup and hopped on. She clicked for Prince Albert to walk forward. She signaled for him to jog, which was about the same as an English trot. He did it with no problem.

"He wants only *you* to ride him," Daphne observed after Taylor had jogged once around the corral before bringing Albert to a halt. "You're going to have to train him out of that or he'll be no good for lessons."

"How do I do that?"

"I don't know but I'll try to find out," Daphne replied. "Maddy's light. We can try her with Pixie."

"I'll get Pixie ready," Taylor offered as she dismounted.

"We'll come with you," Daphne suggested. "It will be good for Maddy to see the barn and how to tack up a horse."

*   *   *

151

Late that afternoon, Taylor was brushing out Prince Albert's tail in his stall when Mrs. LeFleur joined her. "Pixie did well with Daphne's second student today," she said, reaching in to pet the pony in her next-door stall.

"She did great," Taylor confirmed.

Mrs. LeFleur moved over to Prince Albert's stall. "But this guy did *not* do so well," she remarked. "When I asked, Daphne told me he only seemed to want you."

"I'll train him not to be that way," Taylor said quickly.

"What if you can't?" Mrs. LeFleur asked.

"I will. There's got to be a way. Daphne is going to see what she can find out about it."

"I hope it doesn't take too long."

Taylor didn't like the sound of this. "Please give me the chance to try, Mrs. LeFleur. Please. I'll work with him every day for as long as it takes."

"Before you panic, Taylor, I received a phone call today that gave me an idea that might solve the problem. If Albert could get accustomed to just one more rider, we could lease him to that person."

"Does that mean he wouldn't belong to me and you

anymore?" Taylor asked, preparing to launch a strong objection.

"We'd still be the half owners," Mrs. LeFleur assured her. "The lease would simply entitle that person to be the only other rider allowed to ride Prince Albert. In turn, the monthly payment would contribute to his food and board."

"That sounds okay," Taylor admitted. "Ralph Westheimer sometimes did that at his ranch. Who called?"

"A woman was interested in the lease for her daughter. Oh, what was the name? It was odd . . . some kind of fruit."

Taylor's throat went dry. "A fruit?" she croaked.

"Yes. Plum! That was it. The daughter's name was Plum."

Chapter 16

"I just want you to get to know Prince Albert and Pixie," Taylor said to Travis as they sat on the bus the next day after school. "Daphne asked one of the instructors at Ross River Ranch about Prince Albert and —"

"When did he become a prince?" Travis asked.

Taylor explained about the coincidence of the nameplate. "It's a better name, don't you think?"

"It's kind of goofy, if you ask me," said Travis, bluntly honest as usual.

"Well, I like it," Taylor insisted. "Anyway, the instructor at Ross River said that obviously Prince Albert has had some bad experience with someone — probably the guy with the baseball cap — and now he only trusts me. But if he gets to know other nice, kind people, he'll rebuild trust."

"I'm a guy, remember. He hates guys."

"But that could change," Taylor argued.

"Forget it. I'm not riding a horse."

Taylor sighed with frustration. "This has to happen fast. I've convinced Mrs. LeFleur to wait another week. I can't let Plum lease Prince Albert."

When Taylor got home that afternoon, Claire and her mother were sitting at the kitchen table. Recipe books were spread out in front of them. "How was school?" Jennifer asked.

"Okay," she said, tossing her books on a chair. "Plum Mason kept coming over to talk to me. I don't know how much longer I can avoid her."

"She never called me," Claire said. "I don't know how she found out about the ranch."

"It was those stupid flyers I put up," Taylor said. "They led her right to it."

"I'll come by," Claire offered. "At least Albert — excuse me, *Prince* Albert — knows me a little. I'll bring apples."

"Thanks," Taylor said sincerely.

"Do you think Devon Ross's guests would like mousse cups?" Jennifer asked. She'd gotten the catering job at Ross River Ranch and seemed obsessed with developing the greatest lunch she'd ever made.

"A cup of moose meat?" Taylor asked, wrinkling her nose in disgust. "Gross."

Jennifer and Claire laughed. "No, silly," said Jennifer. "This mousse is spelled differently. It's a kind of pudding. I'd serve it in graham cracker crust cups."

"Oh," Taylor said, embarrassed. "*That* sounds good."

"Okay, I'll do it," Jennifer said, putting a Post-it on the recipe page. "I have two weeks to pull this together."

"Mom, can I help you — for free, I mean — just to help?" Taylor asked.

"And because you're dying to see Ross River Ranch," Jennifer added with a knowing smile.

Taylor grinned. "That, too," she admitted.

"We have to have a business meeting, girls," Mrs. LeFleur said to Daphne, Mercedes, and Taylor later that same afternoon. They were outside the main building. Tradespeople were all around, still painting, scraping, and repairing. "Now that I have Daphne as Head Instructor, Mercedes as Junior Barn Manager, and Taylor as Assistant Junior Barn Manager, we need something else right away."

"What?" Taylor asked.

"Does anyone have an idea for a name for this ranch?" Mrs. LeFleur inquired.

The three girls looked from one to another as they tried to come up with a name.

"Rough and Ready Ranch," Daphne suggested after a moment.

Mrs. LeFleur glanced at the men and women who were still scraping the wood of the main building. Roofers had arrived and were climbing ladders to inspect the damage. "It's more like *very* rough and not-ready-at-all ranch," she commented.

"It'll be ready someday soon," Daphne said. "Think positive."

"You're right," Mrs. LeFleur agreed. "I'll just hope the rest of my money doesn't run out before this place is whipped into decent shape. Anyone else have an idea?"

"Second Chance Ranch," Mercedes offered.

"I like that a lot, but I think I saw others with the same name when I was searching online," Mrs. LeFleur said. "How about you, Taylor? Any thoughts?"

"How about Another World Ranch?" That was how she saw the place — or at least how it could be. It was a place where cranky parents didn't quarrel and worry about money. There was no grouchy old Mrs. Kirchner. No one left a horse and pony to starve in a barn. There was no Plum Mason. "Or how about The Best Place in the World?" she amended.

Mrs. LeFleur smiled and nodded. "It could be the best place in the world, Taylor. If we set our minds to it, we just might make that happen."

Mrs. LeFleur reached inside her barn jacket and pulled out a weathered, crinkled black-and-white photo. It was about the size of a notebook. "Look what I found when I was cleaning up in here," she said, handing the photograph to Taylor. "It was way back in that closet under some moldy old horse blankets."

Mercedes and Daphne came close to Taylor so they could see over her shoulder. The photo showed happy, smiling people, some standing, others on horseback. They were dressed in the style of the late 1920s, or maybe it was the early '30s. Behind them was a large wooden sign. Taylor recognized it as the sign that stood at the entrance to the ranch, its paint now too crackled and faded to read. But in this photo the writing was clear as could be. "'Wildwood Stables,'" Taylor read. "'Trail rides, lessons, boarding, pony rides, and fun for everyone! All horse lovers welcome!'"

"No one has come up with a better name," Mrs. LeFleur said, "so I was thinking we should go back to the original. It has authenticity and charm, don't you think?"

The three girls looked at one another, each checking the other's reaction. "People would be able to find the place," Mercedes said. "It's right here on Wildwood Lane."

"I like it," Daphne agreed.

Taylor thought of all the people, like her father and Mr. Romano, who had such warm memories of the place. They would like having it back just as it was. And riders her age would have experiences just as wonderful. "It's good," she agreed, nodding. "I think it's good."

"That settles it," Mrs. LeFleur stated. "Wildwood Stables it is."

The sound of a bike on the dirt road made everyone turn toward Travis, riding fast toward them. He had a big canvas bag slung over his shoulder. He nearly threw his bike to the side after sliding to a halt. "Don't worry," he cried. "I'm here and I have all my dad's tools. Boy, riding down Quail Ridge Road with tools on my back was *not* easy, and I rode past Wildwood Lane three times. Someone should pull those vines off the sign."

Taylor knew that made sense, but she wouldn't volunteer to do it. Somehow she liked the idea that Wildwood Lane was hidden and hard to find. Though, of course, that wouldn't be too good for business.

"Okay, I'm ready to work," Travis said enthusiastically. Then he noticed all the workers. "Oh, I see you don't need me," he said more quietly.

"We need you," Taylor said quickly, going to his side.

"I'm *not* riding a horse, so forget that," he told her firmly. "There's no way."

"You could just say hi to Prince Albert and Pixie," Taylor coaxed, glancing at the horse and pony grazing contentedly in the nearest of three corrals.

Travis shook his head. "I came here to repair stuff, but you have that covered, so I'll just go."

Mrs. LeFleur came alongside Travis and placed her hand on his shoulder. "Not at all, young man," she said. "We need you very much. You can be our new Junior Head of Buildings and Grounds."

"Does that mean I'm in the Working Student Program Taylor told me about?" Travis asked.

Mrs. LeFleur looked over Travis's head and shot a perplexed, questioning glance at Taylor.

Taylor realized she'd never actually told Mrs. LeFleur that she'd made that program up and advertised it on her flyer.

Taylor nodded to Mrs. LeFleur and the woman didn't question it. "Yes, young man, that's what you're in. And you're a founding member, I might add, sort of an executive," said Mrs. LeFleur.

Travis smiled at Mrs. LeFleur, seeming pleased.

"Now, come with me," Mrs. LeFleur said. "I trust you have a claw hammer in there. There are a number of sharp nails I need yanked out of the box stalls."

Travis looked over his shoulder at Taylor as Mrs. LeFleur guided him toward the stalls in the main building. She grinned and shot him two thumbs-up.

The best place in the world had just gotten even better.

Come back to

WILDWOOD STABLES

Playing for Keeps

Read on for a sneak peek!

Mrs. LeFleur approached the corral leading Albert's friend Pixie, a cream-colored Shetland pony mare, behind her. Seeing Mrs. LeFleur and Pixie together made Taylor notice how alike the pony and the ranch's owner were. Both were short, compact, and just past middle age. Pixie's frizzy, unruly mane seemed like the equine version of Mrs. LeFleur's curly hair. All Pixie needed was a pair of thick glasses and she'd be the pony version of Mrs. LeFleur, Taylor thought.

"Perhaps Prince Albert would be more at ease if Pixie were nearby," Mrs. LeFleur suggested as she opened the corral gate and led the small pony inside.

"Maybe," Taylor agreed.

"Here's your pal, Prince Albert," Daphne said.

Prince Albert went to Pixie and they nuzzled noses affectionately. "They're so sweet together," Daphne noted, and Taylor nodded.

Mrs. LeFleur stroked Prince Albert's side. "How are you today, Your Highness?" she asked him. She looked to Daphne and Taylor. "He doesn't seem to mind me petting him."

Taylor's shoulders tightened. She knew Plum Mason's voice from her eighth-grade class at Pheasant Valley Middle School. Turning, Taylor faced the girl. Plum's diamond stud earrings peeked from her long blonde hair and gleamed in the sunlight. The leather soles of her expensive riding boots were propped on the lower rung of the corral fence, and her elbows were settled on the top.

"You have to show him who's boss," Plum added. "You can't just let him do what he wants. Every good rider knows that."

"He's a little shy of people yet," Mrs. LeFleur told Plum. "We don't want to force him."

Plum shot Mrs. LeFleur a tight smile. "Is that the horse I'm going to lease?"

"Oh, are you Plum Mason?" Mrs. LeFleur inquired.

Taylor's stomach clenched. Mrs. LeFleur had mentioned that Plum's mother had called to inquire about leasing a horse. Since Prince Albert and Pixie were the only animals at the ranch, the quarter horse was all Mrs. LeFleur had to offer.

"No!" Taylor blurted.

Mrs. LeFleur looked at her sharply.

"I mean . . . I'm the only one he'll let ride him, so there's no way he could be leased," Taylor explained, more for Mrs. LeFleur's benefit than for Plum's.

"Excuse us a moment, will you?" Mrs. LeFleur said to Plum. "I need to speak to Taylor a moment . . . privately."